Whispers of Hope

BOOK SEVEN IN THE WHISPERS OF NEW ENGLAND SERIES

SUE MILLS

Choose The Front Row Media

Author's Note

THANK YOU FOR PICKING up Whispers of Hope

This is the seventh book in the Whispers of New England series. After a brief detour in Whispers of Humility, to find out what Norah, Sam's former partner was all about, I return to Caden and his best friends Danny and Rob who were introduced in Whispers of Mistletoe. I've known from the second I wrote that Robbie would not be joining his friends for their usual Friday night drink at O'Malley's Pub, that I would tell his and Jenny's story. And now, several years later, here we are.

The challenge in writing this was balancing story telling with an accurate portrayal of the medical side of an infertility journey. I have tremendous respect for anyone who has traveled that road and I hope any liberties I've taken in the name of story are acceptable.

SUE MILLS

Whispers of Family, coming in November will form a duet with Hope to complete Robbie and Jenny's story. I hope you enjoy.

DEDICATION

To the multitude of people striving to have a child.
May you be successful in building the family you desire.

Playlist

Can't Help Falling in Love – Elvis Presley

Total Eclipse of the Heart – Bonnie Tyler

Oh, Pretty Woman – Roy Orbison

Unchained Melody – The Righteous Brothers

Old Time Rock & Roll – Bob Seeger

Crocodile Rock – Elton John

Blue Cowboy Boots – Karen Waldrup

Country Gold – Josie Sal

Beer Drinkin' Night – Colby Lee Swift

If Barstools Could Cry – Robby Johnson

We Are Family – Sister Sledge

Contents

Chapter One

A Night at O'Malley's

Jenny

ZING! THE DART HIT the bullseye with a resounding *pop*, and Robbie Hatch raised his arm in victory before scrambling through the crowded bar to the table where his beer was waiting. After a long swallow he put his hand on his wife Jenny's back and bent toward her. "I need a kiss for luck, darlin'."

Behind him, someone said, "I need one of those too, darlin'."

Robbie straightened and brushed his unruly blond hair away from his eyes. He glared at his friend Caden in mock anger.

"Keep your mouth off my wife! You can have any woman in this bar. And you know you'll never get the Southern drawl right with that Boston Irish accent of yours, so why do you even try?"

Caden reached for his beer and shook his head. His grin didn't quite reach his deep-blue eyes.

The other woman at the table said, "Either of you could have any woman in this bar."

Caden was tall and well-built with curly black hair. His look was polished compared to Robbie's, who was even taller and wore his blond hair shaggy and slightly long. His eyes were not as dark a blue as Caden's, but both men were handsome and attracted interested glances wherever they went.

"Brooke, you know I only have eyes for Jenny."

"Well, whoever you've got eyes for, you'd better get back to the dartboard, because Danny's looking impatient." Brooke was referring to her husband, who completed the trio of best friends. As they put their glasses on the table, Robbie gave Jenny a quick peck on the lips, and Caden winked at Brooke before he turned to make his way back to the dartboard.

The women laughed as the men walked away.

Jennifer said, "This place is a zoo tonight." O'Malley's Pub was the guys' go-to spot, and the crowd was raucous. The Red Sox had beaten the Yankees in an afternoon game the five of them had attended, and the televisions in the bar were broadcasting Celtics and Bruins playoff games. "Cade seemed good

2

today. Happy?" She wasn't as good at reading Caden's mood as Brooke was.

Brooke started to answer, then said, "Let's go outside, where we can talk without yelling. They'll be throwing darts for a while."

Jennifer nodded and rose from her chair. "I'll tell them what we're doing. Why don't you grab us a table on the patio?" She walked over to the three men and put her arm around Robbie. She leaned in close to his ear. "We can't hear ourselves think in here. We're going to go out on the patio so we can talk. Come join us when you're done."

He gave her a quick hug and said, "Okay." As she walked away, Jen could hear their comments.

"Brooke probably wants to complain about my drinking," Danny remarked.

"No, I'm sure Jenny wants to talk about our unsuccessful baby-making attempts."

She looked over her shoulder as Caden threw the dart he'd been holding and said, "It's either of those, or they want to discuss 'how I'm doing.'" He made air quotes for emphasis. "That's always a hot topic."

Jennifer pushed open the door and located the table where Brooke was sitting.

Brooke said, "This is so much better. I don't know how they come here every Friday night. I much prefer our dinners out."

"Me too. So... Cade?"

Brooke sighed. "I think he had fun with us today. He was like the old Cade." Caden had ended a relationship with a woman he was very much in love with at the end of February and had been miserable for months. "But honestly, he doesn't share much with me, and that's so different from how he used to be. He still hasn't gone into detail about his reason for breaking up with Quinn."

Jennifer said, "If Robbie has any idea, he's not telling me. He was relieved when Cade showed up here two weeks ago. Those two months when he isolated himself—no Friday nights at O'Malley's, no working out or hockey games—that really bothered Robbie. Danny had to have been concerned too."

"Oh yes. But that period knocked up against the changes in the media personnel for the team, so Danny was all tied up in knots about that as well." She looked into the distance. "Truth be told, he's still tied up in knots." Danny was a member of the media team for the New England Patriots.

"Still drinking a lot?"

Brooke nodded.

"I wondered when Caden walked with you to the bathroom."

Brooke laughed. "Well, to be honest, I could have made it to the restroom on my own, but that's Cade, always with the manners. I've told Danny he could take lessons."

"Robbie's Southern-gentleman persona gives Caden's manners a run for their money."

They both laughed, then Brooke said, "Oh, you won't believe this. Cade and I ran into Quinn's friend Sam on our way to the restroom."

"The guy he called the night he broke it off with Quinn?"

"Yeah, I really needed to pee, so I left them alone. Cade seemed... I don't know, happy, maybe... to see him. I know they talked, because Sam was just walking away when I got back."

"I always thought that was so weird for Cade to do, calling Quinn's ex-boyfriend to be with her."

"He didn't want her to be alone. He was doing the same thing we all did for him when everything with Mary blew up."

"Do you ever hear from Quinn?"

The only thing Caden had told his friends following the breakup was that it had been his idea, and he had informed Quinn's former boyfriend, Sam. Both Jen and Brooke had called Quinn to check on her, but she hadn't been forthcoming about why Caden had walked away.

"I've called a few times. She's graduating next weekend, getting her advanced degree."

"We should do something. Send her flowers? I really liked her, and Robbie did as well."

"Flowers are a good idea. Do you want me to take care of it?"

Jen nodded, and Brooke started to say something but got a funny look on her face instead and moved her hand to her belly.

"Are you okay?"

"Yeah, yeah, I... The baby just moved. It's the first time I've felt her. Danny's sure it's a girl." She looked stricken and reached out to place her hand on top of Jennifer's. "I'm sorry."

Jen scoffed. "Don't be ridiculous! That's exciting. Have you decided if you're going to find out?"

A smile filled Brooke's face, but sympathy flowed from her eyes. "It is, but I don't want to make you feel bad. It's going to happen for you. I know it will. We're going to be surprised this time."

Jennifer and Rob had been trying to have a baby since the previous summer.

She sighed. "I know. I've got a doctor's appointment next week. It's only been eight months, and the prevailing wisdom is not to worry until it's been a year. But you know, we're almost thirty-three. In another two years, I'll be at 'advanced maternal age.' We're hoping for more than one, so I'll definitely fall into that designation for any future babies." She took a sip of her wine and stared at her glass as she put it back on the table. "But honestly, right now, I'll be thrilled with one. I'm hoping the doctor will do something on Wednesday."

The door to the pub opened, and the three men came out, each holding a shot glass. Robbie slid into the chair next to Jenny and put his hand on her leg. "Celtics and Bruins both won."

Danny took the chair next to Brooke. "We got us a trio of triumphs!"

Caden pulled a chair from one of the other tables and lifted his glass in a toast. "To winning!" The five of them touched their glasses together, sharing smiles.

Danny took Brooke's hand and leaned over to nuzzle her neck.

She grasped his hand and moved it to her belly then said softly, "I just felt her move a couple of minutes ago."

Danny's face blossomed with a wide smile, and his mouth moved from her neck to her lips.

Robbie rubbed Jenny's shoulder, and she leaned against him, watching Caden gaze at them. She could read his longing.

"I've got to shove off. I'm on duty at seven tomorrow." He was an attending physician in the emergency department at Mass General.

As he stood, the others joined him. They walked to the curb to wait for the rideshares they had called.

Caden grinned. "This is when I most like my brownstone. By the time your rides arrive, I'll be almost home." His house was a short walk away. He leaned in to kiss first Brooke, then Jen on the cheek. Then he fist-bumped Danny and Rob and said, "This was a good day. Thanks!" He loped off into the warm spring night.

Chapter Two

Rekindled Passion

Robbie

DANNY AND BROOKE'S CAR arrived first, and as they climbed in, Robbie said, "Y'all have a nice night." He put his arms around Jenny. "Alone at last. You're lookin' sexy in that jersey, darlin'."

Jenny had her hair pulled back into a ponytail through the hole in her Red Sox cap. Her green eyes gleamed as she said, "You look pretty sexy yourself, sir." They were both wearing the jerseys of their favorite Red Sox players, and it was easy to see why people called them Barbie and Ken, with their tall height, good looks, and blond hair. "I'm so glad it's baseball season again. Let's go to a lot of games this year."

"We will. It's nice seeing you so relaxed."

"Several glasses of wine do that to me." Their ride arrived, and as they climbed in, she said, "I had to drink Brooke's share. She felt the baby move tonight for the first time." She smiled at Robbie.

"Oh, babe."

"It was okay. She felt bad for telling me, and I felt bad that she would want to hide it." She shook her head. "I hate that our friends feel like they have to censor what they say to us for fear of making us sad." She leaned against Robbie. "Enough of that talk. Kiss me."

Robbie murmured, "You don't have to ask me twice." He lowered his lips to hers, and she opened her mouth, inviting his tongue to explore. They kissed all the way home, and Robbie thought about how long it had been since they'd been spontaneous like that. *Is this going to last, or will it dry up when we walk into the house?* Their lovemaking had become mechanical as they concentrated on the best time to conceive and the best position to deliver sperm to egg.

They were barely through the door when Jenny grabbed his hand and dragged him toward the stairs. At the bottom, Robbie pulled her to a stop and enveloped her in his arms. He grabbed her cap, then dropped it to the floor, before lowering his mouth to hers. He kissed her roughly, pushing his tongue into her willing mouth while moving his hand to her back, pulling her closer to him. Jenny moaned softly, then moved away from him. Running lightly up the stairs, she looked back, inviting him to chase her.

In their bedroom, she reached up to undo her ponytail and was shaking her hair free when Robbie crashed through the doorway. He grabbed the bottom of her jersey and pulled it over her head.

She was wearing a lacy white bra, and he drew in a sharp breath. "You know I love it when you go for that innocent look." Pushing one cup below her breast, he took her nipple between his teeth.

Jenny thrust toward him, inviting him to take more.

They moved toward the bed, and when they reached it, Robbie sat on the edge, pulling her onto his lap. Reaching behind her, he unhooked her bra and tossed it away. While his head was buried between her breasts, she tangled her fingers in his hair. He looked up. "I love you so much."

She smiled. "I know. I love you too."

Robbie lowered her to the mattress and moved his hands to the top of her jeans. He unbuttoned them and pulled the zipper down then stood and moved to the bottom of the bed, where he tugged on her pants. She shimmied her hips to help, and when her jeans were off, he ran his hands up her legs. His fingers snaked into her panties, which were white and lacy like her bra. His cock had been hard since they started kissing on the drive home, but seeing her like that lit a fire. "You know what the white lace does to me. Was this deliberate?" His voice was husky with desire, and he adjusted his hips, trying to make room in his jeans.

"It crossed my mind when I was dressing." Her voice was low. "I knew I'd be pretty hot after watching the players in their tight baseball pants all afternoon, and I wanted to ensure that you were in the same place."

"You know that's never a problem, darlin'." His fingers found her clit, and she jumped in response.

He stroked her lightly, and she thrust against him, trying to increase the pressure. His hand moved away, and she frowned at him with her eyes wide. "Calm down. Calm down. As much as I hate to, I've got to get these out of the way." He yanked the panties off and tossed them onto the bed.

Robbie's fingers returned to her folds, and he cautiously dipped his head toward his hand. *She hasn't been interested in me going down on her in ages. Dare I hope?* He leaned in to kiss her mound, and when she squirmed in response, he replaced his fingers with his mouth. His tongue worked her clit, and her squirming grew more pronounced. Raising his head he asked, "You okay?"

Jenny's eyes were hooded as she nodded and murmured, "Mm-hmm."

He returned to licking her and inserted two fingers. "You're so wet."

"Mm-hmm." She wrapped her legs around his head, pinning him in place.

The pressure of his tongue and the thrusting of his fingers increased. He'd made love to her enough to know when she was close, and he wanted to feel her come that way. It had been too long.

"Oh, babe, yes. Don't stop. Make me come."

Robbie took her clit between his teeth, sucking hard as he felt the waves move over her. He slowed his fingers, but left them buried inside until the spasms stopped.

She relaxed her legs, and he raised his head to look at her again.

Smiling contentedly at him, she asked, "Why are you still dressed?" She scrambled to a sitting position next to him and unbuttoned his jersey, yanked it off, then pulled his T-shirt over his head. Her mouth moved to his nipples, and she bit one gently.

He shifted his hips, desperate to find room for his swollen cock.

Jenny moved her hand down and stroked him through his jeans.

He moaned as he thrust toward her.

She unzipped the jeans. "Dammit, I can never get the button."

Robbie grinned and quickly dealt with it.

She slid her hands inside, reaching for the head of his cock.

Savoring the feel of her fingers he jumped off the bed and pushed his jeans and boxers to the floor. As he stood in front of her, she looked approvingly at him.

Reaching around, she gripped his butt and pulled him closer. She took his cock in her mouth while one hand left his butt to stroke the shaft.

"Ohhh, Jenny."

She continued to suck and stroke him as he tried to restrain from thrusting toward her. He didn't want it to end too soon.

Then Jenny stopped and said, "Lie down." When he gladly obeyed, she sat next to him. Grinning, she picked up the white panties he'd taken off her then wrapped them around his cock and stroked the full length of his shaft.

Robbie groaned. "Oh my God, you're going to kill me." He was hotter than he could remember being in a very long time.

Jenny played with him, speeding up the stroking until he was close then slowing down to let him regain control. Finally, she stopped and climbed on top of him, positioning his cock between her legs and rubbing her clit against it. She still had the panties in her hand, and she rubbed them over his chest.

He tweaked her nipples, and she reached down to guide his cock into her.

She took him in fully and stopped to look at him. "How do you want it? Fast or slow?"

"Darlin', at this point, it doesn't matter. I'm not going to last more than a minute."

She laughed and moved up and down on him. "I'm pretty hot myself. But you know, there's something you could do..."

He didn't let her finish the sentence as he quickly shifted on the pillow so that he was half sitting and pulled her toward him. He took her breast in his mouth, sucking hard.

"Yeah, that."

As he sucked, he thrust into her, and she finally started moving against him again. They went at each other in a frenzy until Robbie exploded.

Jenny continued to move until she climaxed. "Ohhh, Robbie." She sighed and collapsed onto him.

He put his arms around her, holding her tightly. When his heart rate returned to normal, he rolled them onto their sides.

After a few minutes, he said, "Maybe we should buy season tickets."

Jenny laughed, as he'd known she would, and he joined her, feeling better after their lovemaking than he had in months. He got up and went to the bathroom then returned with a warm washcloth, which he used to gently wipe away the stickiness, then returned it to the bathroom.

When he came back, Jenny had moved to make room for him, and he crawled under the covers beside her.

"Come closer. I want to hold you."

When she settled her head on his shoulder, he stroked her hair. "Cade was right. This was a good day."

Chapter Three

Reflections and Revelations

Jenny

JENNY REACHED FOR ROBBIE when she awoke, but found his side of the bed empty. She lay quietly for several minutes, thinking about their lovemaking the night before. The memory of it made her clit throb again. It had always been like that with Robbie. When they met, she'd been twenty-four and had ended a long-term relationship six months before. Jenny had been with other guys on a more casual basis, so she wasn't inexperienced, but from the first time Robbie made love to her, she felt like she was being introduced to a whole new world.

Robbie walked in with two steaming cups of coffee, and she scrambled to a sitting position to take one.

He crawled into the bed and gently kissed her. "Good morning."

She loved reconnecting on the weekend. "Good morning to you. How are you feeling?" They'd both consumed a lot of alcohol during the game and at O'Malley's. She was shocked she didn't feel hungover.

"Not too bad. Bit of a headache when I got up. It was that damn shot of Jameson that Caden and Danny insisted on."

She shook her head as she grinned at him. "Peer pressure gets you every time. You should know better."

"I know. I know. How about you?"

"Surprisingly, I feel fine."

"It must have been that superior sex when we got home." He took a sip of his coffee.

"Superior, huh?"

"Are you going to tell me it wasn't?"

"No, it was outstanding." She paused. "It's been a while since we've gone at it with that much abandon." She frowned. "And I know that's probably on me. My focus has been on the timing and—"

He put his finger on her lips. "Stop. We both want a baby, so we've both been concerned about doing it at the best time in the optimal position. It's not your fault." He moved his finger away from her mouth. "But if the heat generated has any effect on conception, then we've surely got quintuplets coming."

They laughed, and she said, "If only it worked that way."

Robbie had his arm over her shoulders, and he stroked her hair. "What's on your agenda for today? I hate to do this, but I had an email this morning that one of my guardian ad litem kids was moved to a new foster home yesterday. I kinda want to check on him. Would you mind? I'd be gone an hour or two at the most."

"Of course I don't mind. We both know how much those kids need you." She turned and kissed him. "I've got all the regular stuff to do to get ready for the week. We'll go for our walk when you get home?" They tried to go for a long walk every Sunday.

"Absolutely! Let's have some breakfast, then I'll head out."

After Robbie left, Jenny got in the shower and, as the water cascaded over her, she smiled, thinking about his involvement with the guardian ad litem program. Eight years earlier, he had walked into the neighborhood center where she was doing an internship as the final piece of her degree program. She was weeks away from getting her master's in social work and trying to decide whether to stay in Boston or return to Minnesota, where her family lived.

Robbie had been dressed in a T-shirt and dark-wash jeans that hugged his narrow hips and long legs. His blond hair was longer than he currently wore it, and Jenny thought he looked like he should be carrying a surfboard. His blue eyes collided with her green ones, and she felt a tingle as he looked her up and down.

Before he could say a word, she asked, "Did you take a wrong turn on the way to California?"

"Uh, California? Why would I be going to California?"

She detected a slight Southern accent. "Aren't you looking for a beach to surf on?"

"No." He looked confused. "Can y'all tell me where to find the director's office?"

"What do you want with the director?"

"My professor told me to talk to her about volunteering here."

"Your professor?" After spending the entire semester at the center, she was used to the steady stream of college students looking for a volunteering gig to pad their resumes. They came dressed in their career-advancing best clothes, and most of them only lasted a week or two. The inner city was not for the faint of heart. "What college are you from?"

"Harvard Law School." His look challenged her to come back at him.

"You don't look like a lawyer."

"Well, I'm not quite there yet. One more year of law school. Would I be more acceptable if I were wearing a suit and tie, darlin'?"

Jenny blushed.

He continued, "I thought the kids might be more comfortable with casual attire. Now, the director's office?"

"Down this hallway, second door on the right." As he started walking, she called after him, "Don't turn left. You'll end up on a California beach, and you forgot your surfboard."

He stopped for a second, started to turn around, then raised his arm with a wave instead.

She had watched him until he reached the director's open door.

Jenny stepped out of the shower, smiling at the memory. *He was so sure of himself. And I was so smitten.* As she dried her hair, she thought more about that day.

She had been almost ready to leave when he finally walked out of the director's office. He'd been with her much longer than most prospective volunteers, and she heard laughter, which was unusual. He headed directly for the door, and she wondered about his abrupt departure, disappointed that he hadn't stopped to talk to her on his way out.

A couple of minutes later, as she was closing her laptop, the door opened, and when she looked up, he was walking back in.

He stopped in front of her desk. "Do you live nearby?"

She narrowed her eyes and asked warily, "Why?"

"I wondered about the parking situation. Do you drive here?"

"I don't drive anywhere in the city! You actually want to drive your car?"

"I need to get to my job across town at the end of the day, and I'm not sure the T will get me there in time. Having my car would make it easier."

"Sorry, I can't help. I use the T or take a rideshare. How often will you be here?"

He grinned. "Three days a week. Serving as a mentor and advocate for the kids. The director liked my T-shirt."

She sputtered. "I didn't *not* like your shirt. You just aren't dressed like most people who come in looking to volunteer."

"You'll find out I'm not like most people, darlin'." And with that, he turned to leave again. He stopped at the door. "Would you like to get something to eat?" Her wariness showed, and he said, "I saw how you deflected my question about where you live. I might be a serial rapist, and you don't want me to be able to track you down."

She continued to look at him with hesitation in her eyes.

"That was wise. I'm glad you watch out for yourself, but I assure you I'm harmless. I really did just want to know about the parking situation, but now… I'd like to get to know you." He extended his hand. "Rob Hatch."

"Jennifer Hagen. We don't want to eat around here. It's not the best neighborhood."

"Suggest a destination. I'm open to anything."

She was jittery, still hesitant.

"The blue line will get us to my neighborhood, and there are lots of fine restaurants there. I'll get a rideshare to take you home after. Send your two best girlfriends a text that you're getting a bite to eat with this incredibly handsome surfer you met today. Let them know you'll text the name of the restaurant in thirty minutes." His eyes twinkled at her.

"Are you always this persistent?"

"No."

She did what he suggested, texting her roommate and her best friend. They walked to the T stop, and he told her where they would get off. She smiled because it was the stop she took to get to her apartment. He suggested a pub she'd been to many times. As they walked in, the hostess greeted them by name.

After they sat down, Robbie asked, "You've been here before?"

"I have. My apartment is nearby."

He raised a hand. "Stop. Don't tell me where. Not till you know me better."

She laughed. "Do you live close by?"

"I do. But I'm not telling you where because I'm not sure that you aren't a serial axe murderer."

She rolled her eyes.

"Are you going to text your friends to let them know where we are?"

"If I do that, they'll come to check you out."

"I'm not scared. They'll be impressed."

"Cocky much?"

"I prefer to think of it as self-confident."

"Where'd the Southern accent come from?"

"I lived in Tennessee from three to fourteen, then my family moved up here. I fell in love with Boston and stayed when they moved to the Pacific Northwest two weeks into my senior year."

"Where'd you live?"

"A friend's family took me in. We went to Boston University together. Now, he's in med school, and I'm in law school. We share a place. So I'm not cocky, but I've been on my own for quite a few years, and I am sure of myself. I'm not hearing any Boston in your accent. Where's home?"

"Minnesota. I'm just finishing up my master's degree at Simmons."

"What's next?"

"I honestly wish I knew. My internship finishes in two weeks, and my lease is up at the end of June. I'm trying to decide whether to stay here or go home."

Her hand was resting on the table, and as he gazed into her eyes, he put his hand on top of it. "You should stay here. I'm looking forward to working with you at the center. Ms. Smith said you've been working as a mentor and advocate, just like I will be. I think we'd make a dynamite team."

"What brought you to the center? There are dozens of places you could volunteer that would be more convenient and more relevant to a law career."

"You, darlin'. You led me there."

"Oh my God." She laughed.

"I've got this pathological need to give back." He had shrugged. "I have no idea where it comes from."

Jenny put her hair dryer down. *And with that, I fell in love with him.*

When Robbie got home, they set out for their Sunday walk. He started out at a much more aggressive pace than usual, and Jenny scrambled to keep up with him.

After a few minutes, he opened up. "Do people have any idea of the trauma they inflict on kids? This was the fifth move for Elliott in less than a year. It's bad enough that his parents are crackheads, but why do people sign up to be foster parents if they don't intend to provide a long-term, stable home for a child? He's not a bad kid. Five moves, Jenny! It makes me so angry!"

When she took his hand, he slowed his pace. "I'm sorry. I don't want to bring our Sunday down."

"It's okay. It's who you are and one of the things I love about you. I was thinking earlier about the day we met."

"That summer was so magical. Being at the center together and all those nights you came to the bar to watch me work."

"Then moving in with you and Caden after Danny and Brooke got married. It's a good thing Cade was subsidizing us, because I couldn't afford anything with the tiny salary I got from the center. Speaking of Cade, he sent a text that he wants us to come to his place for dinner on Saturday along with Danny and Brooke. What do you think is up with that?"

"No idea. It should be fun, though. We always have a good time at his place."

"I hate the way your bro code keeps you and Danny from sharing anything about Cade with Brooke and me. You haven't even told me why he broke up with Quinn."

"Because I don't know. He hasn't told us anything. There's no bro code." He smiled at Jenny. "We're manly men! We don't talk about our feelings." They laughed because Robbie was very willing to share his feelings.

They went by a park that had exercise equipment, and they worked out at each station. After the last one, they went to the swing set. "So, you're going to see your doctor on Wednesday. Are you sure you don't want me to go?"

"I don't think it's necessary. We'll probably just talk. And she'll tell me to come back in September when it's been a year."

"If you change your mind, just let me know, darlin'. I can rearrange my schedule."

They were almost home when Robbie said, "You know, we haven't made any vacation plans for this summer."

Jenny answered, "Because we thought I'd be eight or nine months pregnant or, even better, that we'd have a newborn." She shook her head, and Robbie took her hand. "Do you have any ideas?" In the past, they had taken extravagant vacations to Europe and Australia.

"One of my colleagues has a cabin on Lake Winnipesaukee in New Hampshire. He's shown me pictures. It's beautiful. We could swim, kayak, or go biking. I think it would be good to get away for a week."

"I'd be up for that. Can you see if it's available in July?"

"I will. And I'll try to find a week when the Sox are on a road trip, since we're going to be going to all the home games."

She laughed, and he pulled her in close, leaning down to kiss her.

Chapter Four

Caden's Secret

Robbie

Monday was Robbie's day to make dinner, and he opted for takeout from their favorite Italian place.

Jenny walked in to find the table set and the food waiting. "Yum, this is a nice surprise."

"Caden is coming over at seven. He said he needs some legal advice."

"That's kind of cryptic."

"Yeah, I thought so too."

After they finished eating, he was helping Jenny clear the table when a sharp knock came on the door, and Caden entered.

He kissed Jen on the cheek and said, "It's good to see you."

"Twice in less than a week," she answered. "It's nice. We've missed you."

"I know. Are you going to make it on Saturday?"

"We wouldn't miss it. Dining on your rooftop terrace is one of the joys of summer."

"I'm sorry to take the big guy away from you tonight. I won't take up much of his time."

"It's okay. I've got a bubble bath calling my name." Jen headed upstairs, leaving Caden and Robbie in the kitchen.

Robbie watched as Caden squeezed his eyes shut and wondered where his friend had gone. "Caden." Robbie tapped his shoulder. "Should we go to my study? You said you need some legal help. Am I going to need to take notes?"

Caden nodded. "The study sounds good. What I have to say is short and sweet. You won't need notes."

Robbie's study had hunter-green walls and dark woodwork. Shelves holding his law books lined two sides, and a large desk sat in the corner. Caden sank into one of the brown leather chairs while Robbie poured them each a shot of Irish whiskey. "Turning me on to Jameson may be one of the worst things you ever did to me. I had such a headache Sunday morning."

Caden smiled. "Yeah, me too. Not sure it was just the whiskey, though. The beers consumed may have contributed as well." He ran a hand through his hair. "How are things on the baby-making front? Still no luck?"

Robbie studied Caden before answering. The question irritated him, and he struggled to keep his voice civil. "Is that what you came here for? To ask me if Jenny's pregnant? If you hadn't completely disappeared on us for two months, you'd know she isn't."

"I'm sorry. I wasn't fit company for anyone, not even myself. And I'm sorry she's not pregnant yet. I know how much you both want a child."

"Yeah, it's rough." Robbie's tone softened. "It hasn't been a year yet, so if she questions her doctor, the answer is always just to keep trying. That Brooke gets pregnant just by Danny looking at her doesn't make it any easier. But seriously, that's not why we're sitting in my study, is it?"

"No. I'm going to Honduras for two months to work at a medical mission. I leave in a couple of weeks."

Surprised, Robbie raised his eyebrows. Caden had never spent more than a week away from Boston.

"It's why I invited you all for dinner on Saturday. I'm going to tell the others then."

"Whoa, I was not expecting that. How come I'm so privileged to find out first?"

"I.... I want to change my will."

"That's not my area of expertise."

"I know. I know. Just hear me out. What I want is simple. I'd rather not use my usual lawyer, and I don't have time to find another one and meet with them before I leave. I'm hoping if I tell you what I want, there's someone at your firm who can take care of it for me."

"We have a division for estate planning." He reached for a pad of paper. "I definitely need to take some notes."

"No, you really don't. I want to leave everything to Quinn."

Rob shook his head. "You want to do *what*?"

"I want a will that leaves everything I have to Quinn."

"What about your family?"

"What about them? Rob, we all have far more money than any of us will ever need."

Caden's grandfather had been killed in a construction accident years earlier, which had resulted in a multimillion-dollar settlement. He had established trust funds for Caden and his sisters before he died, leaving them all with a sizable inheritance. Rob was well aware of Caden's uneasy relationship with the money. He felt guilty about having so much that he hadn't earned and was wary of new people who befriended him for fear that they were using him for his money.

"Everything? The brownstone, the car? Is where you're going dangerous? I mean, are you likely to get killed? Jesus, Cade!"

"No, not all that dangerous, but planning for this made me think. I could walk across the street and get hit by a bus. I've been considering this for a while, and now's the time to do it."

"Are you going to tell her?"

He shook his head. "I'm not. I'm not in communication with her. Likely, nothing will happen to me, and she'll never even know. If something happens, I'm sure you'll be able to explain it to her."

Rob sat for several minutes, rolling the shot glass between his hands. "Cade, why not? It's obvious how much you care about her. You're talking about giving her millions of dollars."

Caden walked over to the bar and refilled his shot glass. He knocked back the whiskey before he turned to Rob. "I can't. You don't understand. You don't know what I did."

"So tell me. Make me understand. Jenny thinks we have some kind of bro code going on because when she asks how you are, I tell her I don't know. She doesn't believe you haven't told Danny and me anything. What happened, Cade? We used to share every detail of our lives."

Caden picked up the bottle of whiskey and started walking toward Rob then stopped and pivoted back to the bar, where he put down the alcohol and picked up two bottles of water. He sank back down into the leather chair and tossed one of the bottles to Rob. He took a long swallow of the water before he spoke. "When I see Quinn with another man or I even think about her with another man, pictures of Mary riding that rando flash in my head. My ears ring, and I can't breathe. I lose my mind."

Rob pondered his words then said, "You know how often I've seen PTSD proposed as a defense and how overused I think it is, so I don't say this lightly, but that's what it sounds like is happening to you."

"It is. I know it is, but I don't know how to make it stop."

"Aren't you seeing a therapist?"

"Twice a week since February."

"Quinn would understand. She'd help you work through it."

"No!" Caden ran his hand through his hair. "I ended it, and it needs to stay ended."

"When have you seen her with another guy? It was obvious to all of us how much in love with you she was. She'd never look at another guy."

"With Danny at the New Year's Eve party."

"Danny? Dude, we all dance with each other. That's harmless. Does Danny know?"

"I was dancing with Brooke, so she saw my reaction, and yes, she told him."

"And that's why you ended it?"

"It's not a one-time thing. And it's escalated. The week before I broke it off, she told me she was late, and I flipped out. The pictures of Mary started flashing, and I could hear Danny telling me she'd been screwing around the whole time we were together. I was wild with the idea that Quinn was having sex with someone else, probably her friend Sam. I walked outside trying to make it all stop. Barefoot. In the snow." He paused, took a long swallow of the water, and looked toward the ceiling. Then he lowered his gaze back to Rob. "I was right at the edge of going at her physically. I won't be that man. Won't be someone who abuses a woman."

31

"You and Quinn can conquer it together."

He shook his head. "No, I don't trust myself." He finished the water. "Can you help me? Please? I'll always love her, and there's no one else I want to leave the fruits of my grandfather's labor."

Rob nodded. "Yeah, I can call in a couple of favors to get it done in the next week. Someone will call you for the details they'll need to get it written." He put down his water bottle. "I had no idea what prompted the breakup. I'm sorry you weren't comfortable sharing that with us."

Caden ran a hand through his hair. "I'm ashamed. You won't believe this." He snorted. "Outside of my therapist, the only person I've 'talked' to is Sam. He texted me after Quinn told him the whole story, and we've been texting off and on since then. Weird, huh?"

Rob nodded. "Kinda."

"I'm marginally better. Coping, I guess. I'm hoping this mission trip will get me out of my head." He stood. "Your beautiful wife is waiting for you, fresh from a bubble bath. You can share this with her. Tell her there's no bro code."

Chapter Five

Prescription? Keep Trying

Jenny

JEN WALKED INTO HER gynecologist's office with trepidation, acutely aware of her flat stomach and envious of the softly rounding bellies of the other women in the waiting room. She watched as a heavily pregnant woman walked in with her partner and sank into a chair. They were called into an exam room before Jen, and she sensed the woman's discomfort as she struggled to get to her feet. The man with her extended his hand to help, and she leaned against him as they left the waiting area.

How I wish that were me. I was fine with Brooke feeling their baby move for the first time, but the sight of a woman so close to giving birth just makes me ache to be there. Tears welled in her eyes, and she blinked rapidly to dispel them.

A nurse took her to an exam room, where she answered questions and underwent the usual weight and blood pressure checks, which were normal. *Normal! God, there's nothing normal about a thirty-two-year-old woman who can't conceive.* She blinked back tears again as Dr. Randolph entered the room.

"I'd ask how you are, but I can see you're upset. What's going on?"

"Nothing. Absolutely nothing. And that's the problem. It's been eight months, and I'm still not pregnant." More tears threatened. "Damn, I don't want to cry. But I'm frustrated!"

"As I told you when we talked a couple of months ago, we rarely get concerned until a couple has been trying for a year."

"I know that's when *you* get concerned, but I'm concerned *now*. We've done everything I've read about to optimize our chances. The first couple of months, it was fun, exhilarating to think that we might make a baby when we made love. And when it didn't happen, I started taking my temperature. We started having sex at the best time and in the recommended positions. And we've still got nothing. It's not fun and exhilarating anymore." She blushed, and the doctor raised her eyebrows. "Saturday, we went to a ballgame, had quite a bit to drink, and for the first time in months, we went at each other like we used to."

"Sometimes, relaxing and not thinking about conception can do the trick."

"Robbie said we'd have quints on the way if the heat we generated had anything to do with it." Jen managed to smile. She'd been going to the same doctor for years and felt comfortable being open with her. "Isn't there anything you can check now to see why I haven't gotten pregnant?"

"Give me a minute to look through your chart." Jen studied the posters in the exam room. She especially liked the one that read "Specializing in tiny human birthdays." After a few minutes, the doctor said, "I'd forgotten that your periods were very irregular prior to going on the pill in college. You stayed on that until last year, when you and Robbie decided you were ready to have a baby. How long before you had a period after stopping the pill?"

"I stopped at the end of July and didn't have a period until the end of September." She grinned ruefully. "We thought we'd hit the jackpot and I'd gotten pregnant on our first try. But since September, they've been like clockwork, every twenty-eight days."

"How heavy are they?"

"Heavier than they were on the pill, but not debilitatingly so."

"It's mid-May, so you've actually been trying for almost ten months. How does this sound? I'll do an internal exam and order some labs to check a few things. I'll step out so you can change."

Jen knew the drill. She'd been diligent about her health since she became sexually active in college. The doctor returned and started the exam. *I'm so glad Robbie didn't come with me. I don't think there's a less dignified position than lying on this table with your legs spread.* The doctor paused her exam and seemed to go back over territory she'd already covered. *This is definitely taking longer than usual.*

The doctor finished and said, "You can sit up."

Jen pushed to a sitting position and asked, "What's up? I can tell by your face that something isn't typical."

"No, I felt something. I'd like you to have an ultrasound. Why don't you go down to the lab for the blood draw then come back to the waiting room? I'll see when we can get it scheduled."

When Jen came back, the nurse she'd seen earlier led her back to the exam room. "We had a cancellation and can do the ultrasound in an hour if you can wait."

Jen nodded eagerly. "Of course I can wait." She sent Robbie a text letting him know she would be late getting home and would pick up Thai food on the way.

The tech came in more quickly than expected and went over what she'd be doing. It was uncomfortable but not painful, and

Jen was happy when it was finished. She got dressed and waited for the doctor to come back in.

"The ultrasound backed up what I thought. You have some small fibroid tumors. I don't think they're preventing conception. We could remove them, but then you would need to heal from the surgery before you could start trying again to conceive. And that would be several months. I think the better plan is for you to enjoy the summer, and we'll schedule an appointment for right after Labor Day. Maybe it'll be a pregnancy visit, and if not, we'll start a fertility workup."

"You really don't think the fibroids are why I haven't gotten pregnant?"

"I really don't, but we can remove them if that's what you want."

"I trust you, but I want to discuss it with Robbie."

"As you should. I'll call when I have your lab results, and you can tell me what you've decided."

Robbie took the bags from Jenny's arms when she walked in and, after placing them on the counter, gathered her into a hug. He buried his face in her hair. "How did it go?"

"Better than I expected. She performed an internal exam, sent me for lab work, then did an ultrasound. I totally thought all we would do was talk today. I have fibroid tumors."

"What does that mean? Is it why you haven't gotten pregnant?"

"She doesn't think so." As they opened the bags and filled their plates, she shared everything the doctor had told her.

Robbie poured each of them a glass of wine. "I like the idea of enjoying the summer. And I'm not wild about you having surgery or that we'd then need to wait before trying again."

"You don't want to go any period of time without having sex." She grinned at him.

"Do you?" Their sex life was very active. They seldom went more than a few days without making love.

She shook her head, agreeing with him.

Jenny was standing at the counter, taking care of the leftovers, when Robbie came up from behind and put his arms around her waist. He nibbled on the back of her neck, and she shuddered in response.

He whispered, "I bought us a present today."

Jenny spun around, excited that he had a surprise for her. "What? What did you buy?"

He reached into his pocket and pulled out an envelope. "Season tickets for the Sox."

"You did not!"

He grinned at her. "Oh yes, I did."

"Let me see." She grabbed for the envelope, which he was holding just out of her reach. "Come on." She jumped, trying to snatch it away from him. Unable to, she put her hands on his ribs and started tickling him.

He lowered his arms to defend himself, and she grabbed the envelope. He laughed as he said, "You don't fight fair."

Jenny tore the envelope open and pulled out the tickets. "Oh my God, you did!" She threw the tickets onto the counter and launched herself into Robbie's arms. He lifted her, and she wrapped her legs around his waist. Smashing her lips against his, she thrust her tongue into his welcoming mouth.

Robbie lifted her higher and turned so he could set her down on the island. They continued kissing until he stepped back and reached for the bottom of her shirt. She raised her arms so he could pull it off.

Her bra was navy, and as he reached around her to unhook it, he asked, "Are you wearing the navy thong?"

She nodded, with her eyes twinkling.

He leaned into her, taking one breast in his mouth while he pinched her other nipple.

Jenny sighed, "Oh, Robbie."

He raised his head and, holding her at arm's length, asked, "So you like the surprise?"

"I love it! Now come back here."

She tugged at him, and he gave her a kiss before lifting her off the counter. He carried her upstairs, and when they reached the bedroom, she slid out of his arms, onto the floor. He'd changed into sweatpants before she got home, and when she tugged on them, they fell easily into a puddle at his ankles. "Ooh, commando." She raised her eyebrows at him. "Were you expecting something?"

He grinned. "Me? Expect something? Just trying to be comfortable, darlin'."

"Uh-huh." She pushed up to her knees and reached around him to stroke his butt.

He squirmed in response, and his cock thickened. She stuck her tongue out and licked the head. When he took a step toward her, she wrapped her lips around him. He sighed and, with her hands still on his butt, she pulled him even closer. She could tell he was struggling not to thrust into her mouth. She took him deeper while she moved her hand around and stroked the shaft.

Robbie put his hands into her hair, holding her close as she sucked and stroked him. He groaned as his cock grew harder. "Jenny, I'm close." Her lips stayed wrapped around him, and he said, "So close."

She pulled her mouth away just as he exploded all over her. Panting, he sank to the floor beside her.

Jenny put her hand on the side of his face. "I thought I was going to swallow this time." She shook her head, exasperated. "I've got some kind of block against it. I just can't do it."

Robbie took her hand and kissed her fingers. "Darlin', I keep telling you, it doesn't matter. Do I look disappointed?" He drew a finger along her chest. "If we judge by the mess I made, I'm damn satisfied. Don't move." He went into the bathroom and returned with a warm washcloth and gently wiped it over her. Setting the washcloth aside, he drew her against him. He buried his face in her hair, staying still for several minutes until he stood and settled them both on the bed. "I love you so much. Why do you obsess about this?"

"Because I know it was something you did... and liked."

"In college, Jenny! In college! Eons before I met you. We all experimented when we were twenty. Then I grew up. And even better, I met you. Making love with you is everything I ever wanted."

"Not everyone stopped doing that after college."

"What did you do?" He rubbed his forehead. "Read some article in a magazine about how to please a man? Come on. You don't need that. I can't believe stuff like that still gets published."

"No magazine article. I...." She stopped, but she could see the question in Robbie's eyes. "Just forget it." She leaned in to kiss him.

"Oh, no, no, no. Something put this in your head. What was it?"

"Brooke and I have talked about it."

He threw his head back. "Oh my God. You two talk about... that? She and Danny still do... I'll never be able to look at them again."

Jenny collapsed in laughter. "They do more than that. You lived with them. You know what their sex life was like. Is this a throwback to your religious upbringing?"

"Damn, it probably is. I'll never escape my family. Come here. I need to banish those rules." He kissed her aggressively and reached for her clit. "But promise you won't tell Brooke what we do."

She raised her right hand. "I solemnly swear, counselor." She pushed his head toward her breasts. "Now make love to me."

Chapter Six

A Fourth of July Surprise

Jenny

JENNY PULLED ON NAVY shorts and topped them with a red-and-white-striped tank top then studied herself in the mirror. *Appropriately patriotic.* She pulled her hair into a ponytail and put on her navy Red Sox cap.

Robbie came in from a run and looked appreciatively at her. "I need a shower, but I'll be ready to leave soon."

Half an hour later, they walked out the door on their way to Caden's parents' condo. They hosted a brunch every Fourth of July and always invited Robbie and Jenny. He had spent so much time at their house that they regarded him as their second son. Robbie was wearing red board shorts and a navy polo shirt. Jenny bumped against him as they walked. "You never found that surfboard."

He laughed. "The waves aren't very good in Boston. I haven't missed it."

At the waterfront, they were quickly buzzed into Sean and Maureen Brady's condo. As they walked out of the elevator on the top floor of the building, they could hear raucous laughter coming from the end of the hall. Caden's youngest sister, Chrissy, greeted them with a serious expression. "I don't know if I should forgive you for missing my graduation party."

Rob gathered her into a hug. "We were in Minnesota, visiting Jenny's family, darlin'. I promise we'll make it to your college grad party."

"I'm going to hold you to that. There are all kinds of food and drinks scattered around the condo. You know Mom. She's prepared for an army." As Chrissy walked away, Caden's older sister, Claire, walked out of a bedroom holding Rory, her nearly seven-month-old son.

Jen's eyes lit up. "We finally get to meet him. I can't believe he was born in December, and this is our first time seeing him. Can I hold him? Or has he gotten to the 'scared of strangers' phase?"

"He's fine with nearly everyone. He may fall asleep in your arms, though."

"I can't imagine anything better," Jen said as she reached for him. She drew him in close, and he settled into her arms. "Oh, that baby smell is so delicious. Hi, Rory. I'm Jenny, and this is Robbie. We're almost close enough to be another aunt and uncle for you." The baby studied her, and after several seconds, his face broke into a toothless smile.

"I'll take him back whenever you're ready. You've got to eat some of Ma's food. Otherwise, she and Dad will have leftovers for days."

Rob smiled at Claire. "I don't think y'all are getting him back anytime soon. Go enjoy yourself." He touched Rory's head and murmured to Jenny, "He's beautiful. Are you okay if I go get some food and a beer? Do you want something to drink?"

"I'll be fine, and I'd love a glass of wine."

Maureen walked over to Jen and said, "I'm a little partial since he's my first grandchild, but he's so special. I wish the other kids would get going." Maureen Brady's over-the-top interest in children's lives was a legend.

Jen smiled. "With five kids, I'm sure you're going to have more grandchildren than you know what to do with. Has Chloe set a wedding date?" She was one of Caden's middle sisters and had gotten engaged at Christmas.

"Not until next fall. And I know you're right. Plus, I'll have the honorary ones from you, Robbie, Brooke, and Danny. Neither you nor Rob has family here, so Sean and I will be so happy to be surrogate grandparents to your babies."

Jen pulled Rory a little closer before she smiled in response.

Maureen continued, "I wish Cade were with us. Do you think they're celebrating in Honduras?"

"Ma!" Claire interrupted. "He's a big boy. He'll be fine missing one Fourth of July celebration."

"Have you heard from him? We haven't, and he's been gone more than a month."

"No," Claire responded abruptly.

Maureen left when a neighbor called to her.

Claire sat down next to Jen and said, "Bless me, Father, for I have sinned." She grinned. "I lied. I had a text from Cade. Quinn's at the same mission he is. She arrived yesterday."

Jen's eyes widened.

"I know. He was pissed and thought I'd sent her there somehow."

"Did you?"

"No! I knew Quinn was going, but there are several programs in Honduras, so she could easily have landed at a different one. I think it's a bit of serendipity that they're at the same place."

"It is. You don't want your mom to know?"

"God no. I'm sure Cade wouldn't want that."

Robbie wandered back to Jenny and Claire. "Let me hold that little guy for a while. You go get something to eat."

Jenny reluctantly handed the still-wide-awake baby to him.

"Hey, baby. How're you doing? I won't hold you as well as Jenny, but I promise I won't drop you."

Rory responded with a grin.

"You understand me? Are you going to be a prodigy?"

Claire laughed. "Of course he is."

Jen filled a plate and, as she ate, watched Robbie from a distance as he cooed at Rory and stroked his head. *He's going to be such a wonderful dad.* She blinked away a tear. When she finished eating, she went back to the couch and found Rory asleep in Robbie's arms. "You look comfortable." She sat down and nuzzled his neck.

"I am. Except my arm has fallen asleep, and I'm afraid to move."

Claire heard him and reached for Rory. "I'll lay him down. He'll probably sleep for a couple of hours now. You guys are naturals. I didn't hear a peep from him."

Robbie stood, shaking his arm, and reached for Jenny with his other one. He grabbed another beer and a glass of wine before leading her to the balcony overlooking the harbor, which was busy with sailboats and luxury yachts. "Boston does the Fourth up right." He took a long swallow and said, "I want to chat with Cade's other sisters for a bit, then we can head over to Danny's."

She nodded, and they made their way back into the throngs of people.

He whispered into her ear, "I don't recognize many people here. Do you?"

Jenny shook her head. "I miss Cade at times like this."

They located Caden's two middle sisters, and when Maureen came to join their conversation, Jen took her hand.

"You and Sean throw a fantastic party. We're going to Danny and Brooke's for the fireworks, so we've got to leave soon."

Maureen hugged first Jen then Rob, who said, "We had a great time."

Robbie threw his arm around Jenny's shoulders as they exited Maureen and Sean's building. "I didn't think about Claire and James being there with Rory. We wouldn't have gone if I had."

Jenny turned her head to look at him in surprise. "What? Why? I was happy to meet the baby. I can't believe we haven't seen him before this."

"Don't you find it painful? Seeing other people with babies?"

"Robbie, I *love* babies! You know that. I won't avoid them just because we don't have one yet." She returned his skeptical gaze with a challenge in her eyes. "I'm serious. I've even thought about volunteering at the hospital to be a cuddler."

He raised his eyebrows. "A cuddler?"

"Yes! Someone who rocks and cuddles babies to give them extra human touch. Surely you've heard of that."

He shook his head. "Can't say that I have. You really think that's wise?"

"My God, do you think I'm some delicate flower who's going to be wrecked by being around babies because I haven't been able to get pregnant? I'm stronger than that, and you know it." She pulled away and strode toward the T station, slightly ahead of him.

Robbie slowed his pace to give her space to get over being upset.

Suddenly, she whirled around and grabbed his arm. "Robbie! Look! It's Mary!"

"Where?"

She pointed ahead of them at a group of four going around a corner. "Damn, you can't see their faces, but I know it was her."

She was referring to the woman Caden had been involved with for all of his twenties. He'd found her in bed with another man the week before their wedding. She and the man had fled the house, and Caden had never seen her again.

"Do you want to follow them?"

She laughed. "No. I mean, what are we going to do? But wow, it's been three and a half years since we've seen her."

"Did you recognize the people with her?"

"No. She was holding hands with a guy who had a little kid on his shoulders."

"A kid? How old? You think it was hers?"

"Young, maybe three. With curly dark hair." She shook her head in disbelief. "It couldn't be Cade's. Could it?" She looked at Robbie questioningly and took his hand. "Thank God Caden isn't with us."

"You got that right." They started walking again, and he pulled her to a stop. "Darlin', I'm sorry about earlier. It's hard for me to see people with their babies, and I projected that onto you. I shouldn't have."

"I know. It's hard for me, too, but I can't imagine my life without babies in it. If not ours, then our friends' children or little ones in the hospital needing love." She stood on her tiptoes and lightly kissed his lips.

As they walked up the steps to Danny and Brooke's house, the door was flung open, and a flame-haired little boy burst through the opening and jumped into Rob's arms. "Uncle Rob! I thought you'd never get here. I've got a new Lego! Will you help me put it together?"

Rob wrapped his arms around him. "Of course I will, buddy, but can I say hello to your parents first?"

He jumped down and said, "Okay." He turned to Jen and wrapped his arms around her legs. "Hi, Aunt Jen. Do you want to do Legos with us too?"

"Thanks for asking me, Liam, but I think I'll leave that to you and Robbie."

Brooke came to the door and said, "Liam, let them get inside!"

Rob leaned down to kiss her cheek. "Y'all are lookin' pretty good."

Her face flushed. "I'm looking very pregnant. Sorry he attacked you like that."

"Jenny thinks it's because I'm an overgrown child at heart. And the day he stops doing that will be a sad one for me. You got beer around here?"

"There's a cooler out on the deck. Danny's out there with some guys from the team." Danny had developed friendships with several of the players on the Patriots through his job. "It's a smaller crowd than usual because the holiday is in the middle of the week."

Robbie headed toward the deck, and Jen hugged Brooke.

As she pulled away, Jen reached toward Brooke's belly, but hesitated before she touched it. "Okay?"

Brooke took Jen's hand and placed it on her stomach. "Of course. Always. Three more months. This is the best time for me. Past the nausea and not so big yet that everything is a challenge." They made their way to the deck, passing the playroom, where Rob had ended up on the floor, sorting Lego pieces with Liam. He smiled at Jenny as she walked by and raised his beer in a mock toast.

People filled the deck, and Danny was manning the grill. They spent the afternoon eating, drinking, and visiting. The football players understood Danny's anger about not getting the lead media position. They sympathized with him because he deserved the promotion.

Brooke whispered to Jen, "I hope he doesn't get too worked up. It's been months, and I'm tired of hearing about it. I'd like a peaceful day." Liam ran out to the deck with his newly constructed Lego and climbed into Brooke's lap. "He's ready for a nap. I'll be right back."

Robbie grabbed another beer and sat down next to Jenny. "Having fun?"

"I am. It's going to be different watching the fireworks from here instead of being in the crowd at the Charles. I'm excited not to be in that crush of people." In prior years, they had all gone to the banks of the Charles River to listen to the concert put on by the Boston Pops and stayed for the fireworks. It was a rousing, patriotic celebration that they loved, but getting home after was always a struggle. Danny and Brooke had bought their house several months earlier, and it would give them a view of the fireworks, although they'd miss out on the concert. "Brooke is concerned about Danny getting worked up about the job."

Robbie nodded and got up to talk to him.

The house emptied out in the early evening, leaving the two couples to visit while they waited for darkness to fall.

Jen said guardedly, "I didn't want to get into this while everyone was here, but I'm pretty sure I saw Mary when we were on our way here."

Surprised, Brooke asked, "Did she see you? Was she alone?"

"I don't think she saw me, and she was with a guy and another couple. The guy had a small child on his shoulders."

"How small?"

"Young." Jen grimaced. "Two or three. I only saw them for a few seconds. But the kid's hair was dark and curly."

"Like Cade's." Brooke went silent, and Jen knew she was calculating because she had done the same thing.

Danny piped in, "That bitch! Could she have had his baby and not told him?" He went to the cooler for another beer, and when he was seated again, said, "It seriously pisses me off how badly she fucked up Caden."

Jen reached over to put a hand on his arm. "We all feel that way, Danny. Claire told me that Quinn's at the same mission as Caden. Did you know that?"

Brooke nodded. "He texted me yesterday. He's pissed, thinks that Claire or I put her up to it. But we didn't. I swear." She raised her hand like she was taking an oath, and as she did, the sky exploded with color.

Liam raised his arms to Rob. "Will you hold me?" Rob nodded and lifted him so he could see.

The fireworks display lasted half an hour, and when it was done, Liam was asleep.

"Do you want me to take him up to his room?"

Brooke shook her head and looked at Danny.

Danny stumbled as he reached for his son, prompting Rob to say, "I'll carry him. Hate to wake him up. Come on up with me, Dan."

As they walked away, both women heard Danny hiss, "You think I can't carry my kid upstairs to bed?"

Rob placated him by saying, "I know you can, but why wake him up? I don't get to do this, and you can do it anytime."

Jen could sense Brooke's discomfort at how much Danny had drunk. "He'll be fine."

Brooke looked dubious. "I don't know. I hope you're right."

When the men came back, Danny was calmer, and Robbie winked at Jenny as he sat down. They sat at the firepit until Jen could see that Brooke was tired.

As they said goodnight, Rob reminded them, "We won't see you for a couple of weeks. Remember, we're going up to that cottage in New Hampshire next week."

Chapter Seven

Lakeside Retreat

Jenny

AT THE BLEAT OF a car horn, Jenny knew Robbie was back with the rental car. She opened the door and smiled in surprise.

Robbie grinned at her over the roof of the car. "What do you think?"

"A Mercedes SUV. Wow! You've outdone yourself."

They didn't own a car, relying on public transportation and renting if they wanted to leave the city. Robbie took great pleasure in renting upscale vehicles for their outings. They had spent a weekend in Stowe, Vermont, in the fall, and he'd rented a Corvette.

They quickly loaded the supplies they were taking to the cottage and hit the road.

Jenny opened the sunroof as they threaded their way along the interstate. In a short time, they were out of the city traffic and merging into the steady line of cars towing boats or loaded with mountain bikes and kayaks. The sky was sapphire blue, and the air was fresh, free from the oppressive humidity that sometimes plagued New England. Robbie found a radio station playing country rock and cranked the volume. They both sang along for several miles. When they reached the rest area just over the border in New Hampshire, they stopped and took advantage of the large liquor store to stock up for the week.

When they were back in the car, Robbie asked, "Do you still agree that it's wise not to have a car?"

"I do. We leave the city so seldom, and if we had a car, we'd have to pay for garage space. Before Cade started dating Quinn, I bet he didn't take his car out of that garage more than a few times a year."

Robbie nodded in agreement.

"It makes sense for Danny and Brooke because she's traveling all over for her interior decorating gigs and Danny's driving to Foxborough."

"God, remember how parking played a major role in their house hunt?" he asked.

"Yeah, I still can't believe they found a place with a two-car garage."

"I'm glad we agree. I love renting these cool cars when we need one. Hey, this is our exit."

They followed the navigation onto increasingly narrower and narrower secondary roads. Catching glimpses of the lake, they drove along a gravel road and made one last turn that took them to a private driveway, which led to an opening with a spectacular cottage at the water's edge. The lot was totally private, hidden among maple and birch trees. A lush green lawn and flower beds filled with brightly colored plants surrounded the cottage. The building was multilevel with plentiful windows.

Robbie parked the SUV, and they gazed in wonder at the property.

"Oh, Robbie, this is gorgeous! But I don't know if I'd call it a cottage." When he nodded, Jenny continued, "This makes me think so much of Minnesota. I want to lie down and roll around on the grass."

He laughed. "You can do whatever you want. No one is going to see us. Let's unload the car, then we can explore."

They each grabbed several bags, and Robbie punched in the code to open the door. A wall of windows overlooking the lake greeted them. "Whoa, I could learn to like this... a lot."

They put the bags down and opened the sliders that led out to a large deck, which was outfitted with lounge furniture and an outdoor kitchen. A short stairway went from the deck to the lake.

Jenny kicked off her sandals and ran lightly down to the water. She stepped into the lake and walked out until the water was at her knees.

Robbie stayed on dry land. "How is it?"

"Cold. Makes me think of home. Look at all the things for us to play with." She pointed at the kayaks and bikes stored under the deck. "I don't want to bike. There's too much traffic. But I can't wait to get out on the lake in one of those kayaks." As she rejoined Robbie, she noticed a firepit. "We'll be able to make s'mores! And there's an outdoor shower. I've always wanted to try one. We're going to have such a good time."

Robbie took her hand as they walked back into the house. "We can skinny-dip here. It's very secluded." He wiggled his eyebrows at her seductively.

Jenny chuckled before kissing him. "Okay, but we have stuff to do first."

After buying groceries in Meredith, they walked along the waterfront, exploring the sculpture walk erected every summer. They had an ice cream sundae before they returned to the cottage.

Jenny sighed. "That's such a charming little town. There were a ton of people around, but it was so much calmer than Boston. Can't you just feel the tension melting away?"

"I can. Let's go enjoy the deck." Jenny put on a royal-blue string bikini, but as soon as she got to the deck, Robbie reached up to untie the top. "You don't need that, darlin'. Avoid the tan lines."

She pushed the bottom off as well and joined him on the double lounger, lying face down.

He reached over and idly stroked her back then eventually allowed his hand to drift all the way to her butt. "I like this view." He had hardened as soon as she walked onto the deck.

The sun was warm, and there wasn't a cloud in the sky. Jenny murmured she was hot, and Robbie said, "Umm, me too," as he increased his pressure on her bottom.

She jumped up. "Not that way! My body's hot!"

"Oh, it sure is."

"You are incorrigible!" She grabbed his hand, pulling him up. "Let's go in the water."

They raced down the stairs, and Jenny splashed into the water until it was above her waist. "Come on, tough guy. Get out here," she called as Robbie followed more slowly.

He reached her side and said, "I'm shriveled up to nothing."

She laughed and dove under the water to swim out farther.

He watched her, and after a few minutes, she dove under the water again and surfaced with her arms around his waist. "I'm envious every time I see you swim. My doggy paddle is so pathetic." When she shrugged, he continued, "You're going to be in charge of making sure our kids can swim."

She wrapped her legs around him, and he lifted her up. "Your skills show up on frozen water. We both know I can barely stand up on skates. I'm cooled off now. Let's go back to the deck."

He carried her out of the water and up the stairs then sat down on the lounger and took her breast in his mouth, teasing the nipple with his tongue. "You're cooled off, and I'm heating back up."

"It won't take much to get me hot again." She reached for his cock and began stroking it. "And you're not shriveled up now."

He slid a hand between her legs and began fingering her clit.

"Are we doing this out here?"

"Yeah, there's something about the hot sun on your cool skin that's turning me on."

"Scandalous! We've never done this in Boston."

Continuing to stroke him, she leaned down to kiss him. He opened his mouth, inviting her tongue in, and she explored hungrily. He continued fingering her clit and slid a finger inside. She sighed and thrust her hips against his hand.

"You're not cool anymore." He slid her off his lap and onto the lounger.

She opened her legs, and he positioned himself over her, rubbing his cock against her.

"Take me now."

He looked at her with a question in his eyes.

"There's something about being out here. I want you, and I mean now."

"Don't have to tell me twice, darlin'," he said as he filled her up and began moving.

They climaxed together, and he collapsed on top of her, panting. "We can do this again."

She nodded and, when she'd caught her breath, said, "How close do you think the neighbors are? I tried to be quiet."

"We'll walk around and figure that out. I don't want you holding back."

They both laughed and separated to enjoy the sun on their skin.

"We're going to be sunburned where we've never been burned before."

Sunday dawned with bright sunshine in a cerulean-blue sky, and the lake looked like glass, perfect weather for kayaking. Jenny and Robbie paddled along the shore, marveling at the cottages, which were even grander than the one they were in.

They spent the day relaxing on the deck then ventured to Weirs Beach in the early evening. It had a carnival vibe with souvenir shops, arcades, and all kinds of food. They wandered along the docks, where boats ranging from speedboats to luxury yachts were tied up. As darkness fell, the sky exploded with fireworks that were ignited every Sunday night. After the finale, the harbor resonated with the sound of all the boats beeping their horns to express their appreciation.

After stopping for ice cream cones, they walked back to their car. Robbie said, "I really like it here." They passed a kiosk with real estate brochures, and he stopped to take some. "We should think about buying a place. It would be nice to come up every weekend. Or maybe even more."

Jenny slid her arm around his waist. "I like that idea. How often is Doug at the cabin? Do you think we could get another weekend out of him?"

Robbie shrugged. "It won't hurt to ask."

For the next couple of days, they settled into a pattern of eating breakfast on the deck, sunbathing, kayaking, and swimming. In the evening, they watched the sunset, had drinks around the firepit, and made love late into the night.

Wednesday morning, they woke up to driving rain. Robbie lit a fire in the fireplace, and they spent the morning lazily lounging in its warmth. When they got restless, they drove around the lake, exploring the many one-lane roads that led from the main road to the water, then stopped for lunch in Wolfeboro. The vibe there was completely different from the other towns they'd visited. It billed itself as the oldest summer resort in America and was filled with antique shops and historic homes. They found more places they wanted to explore on a return trip. The rain continued all day, and after spending more time by the fire, they went to bed early, enjoying the ping of raindrops on the metal roof.

The sun and warm temperatures returned on Thursday morning, and Robbie awoke before Jenny. He made coffee and took his to the deck.

When Jenny came out, she put her coffee cup on the table before she sat down beside him and took his hand.

He looked at her quizzically. "What's up?"

She bit her lip, gazing into his eyes, seeming hesitant to talk. "I'm late."

"Late for…." Then his eyes lit up with understanding. "Seriously?"

She nodded. "My period has come every twenty-eight days since the end of September, and it is always flowing by eight-thirty. That's why I stayed in bed later this morning. I didn't want to get down here and have to go back upstairs to deal with it."

"Do you want to take a test? Do you have any here?"

"No, I don't even have any at home. After I took so many in August and early September, I decided I wasn't keeping any around."

"We can go to the store."

"I know." She squeezed his hand and took a deep breath. "I don't know if I want to. Part of me wants to remain oblivious. I don't want to see a negative test. I want to think it's possible."

He leaned in and kissed her. "So we won't. But when we get home, let's do it then. You'll be like three days late?"

She nodded.

He put a hand gently on her belly. "I'm not going to lie. The idea that you might be pregnant is making me horny."

"Me too." She moved closer to him and put her arms around him.

"Is it okay to...?"

"Yes." She moved her hand to the front of his shorts, stroking his cock.

He moved against her hand and slid his hand under her shirt.

"Um, no bra. You're making me even hornier." He lifted the shirt and took her breast in his mouth, gently sucking. "You're sure this is okay?"

She moaned lightly. "It's fine. I've checked." With that, she pushed his shorts down and wrapped her hand around his erection. "And now I know I don't have to be quiet. Make love to me, Robbie. Show me how excited you are."

"I'm going to take my time, darlin'. I want to savor this."

They spent the next three days wrapped in a cocoon of expectation. Robbie held Jenny long into the night before letting her roll onto her side so she could fall asleep. On Saturday morning, he brought her a cup of coffee and crawled into bed beside her, where he slid his hand onto her still-flat belly. "Do you have any of the other signs?"

She shook her head. "Not one. But they might not start until closer to five weeks, and if I am pregnant, I'm only about two weeks." She put her hand on his. "It's driving you crazy that I want to wait to take the test, isn't it?"

"A little, but I understand how you feel. And there's something magical about being here with you, knowing it's possible."

They returned to Weirs Beach and went for a tour of the lake on a forty-foot sailboat, where the captain gave them a history class about the lake and shared some myths. Then they stopped at a market and bought lobsters to steam over the firepit. Fresh corn on the cob and salad from a farm stand rounded out their meal. When they finished, they sat by the fire long into the night.

Jenny had settled between Robbie's long legs and, after roasting a marshmallow and popping it into his mouth, she leaned her head against his chest. "I can't think of a vacation that I've been sadder about ending. I've got no desire to return to Boston. Even if we do have three games to go to this week."

Robbie laughed and agreed with her.

Humidity had been building, and Sunday dawned hot and steamy. They took the kayaks out one last time, and after they had them stored under the deck, Jenny removed her bathing suit, took Robbie's hand, and said, "Come on. One last dip in the water."

The drive back to Boston was slow, with all the people returning from New Hampshire and Vermont. Robbie parked in front of their house, and together, they unloaded the car.

As he got ready to return the vehicle, Jenny called out, "Robbie." When he turned, she said, "Do you want to stop at the drugstore? Are you comfortable...?"

"Sure. Don't I pick up tampons for you? Any special brand?"

She smiled. "Whatever looks good to you. How'd I get such an enlightened man?"

"Just lucky, darlin'. Just lucky."

He was gone for over an hour, and Jen burned off her nervous energy by unpacking and starting the laundry.

He walked in carrying a bag and shook it. "I couldn't decide, so I bought three different ones."

She laughed. "That's the move of a teenage boy worried he got his girlfriend pregnant. Although I'm not sure a teenage boy would buy pregnancy tests."

"Whatever. Are we going to do this?"

She took his hand and put it over her heart. "Can you feel that? I'm so anxious!"

"I know. Me too." He wrapped his arms around her. "We'll be okay either way."

She nodded. "You need to let go of me. I've needed to pee since we got home, and I've put it off." She took the bag and went into the bathroom. "Give me a minute, then we'll wait together."

After a bit, she said, "Come on in."

He found her nervously eyeing the test she'd placed on the edge of the vanity. He put his arms around her. "How long do we wait?"

"Three to five minutes."

His leg jiggled as he held her, and he drummed his fingers on her back. "You think it's been long enough?"

"Yes, but I'm scared." She pulled away, and they looked nervously at the stick, which clearly read *Not Pregnant*. Jenny's eyes filled with tears.

"Oh, babe." He wrapped his arms tightly around her again.

She tried to speak, but no sound came out.

He picked her up and went to the bedroom, where he held her as she silently cried.

"I-I thought... really thought this time..." She hiccupped as she spoke through her tears.

"I know. I know. So did I. Should we try one of the other ones?"

She shook her head. "Not tonight. I'll do it in the morning."

Chapter Eight

Reunion at O'Malley's

Jenny

Jen walked into O'Malley's, and her face broke into a smile as she spotted Brooke sitting at the guys' usual table. The two couples had each received a text from Caden letting them know he was back in Boston and that the two things he had missed the most while he was gone were spending time with them and having a beer at his favorite bar. Jen and Brooke had agreed to arrive early so they would have time to talk.

She slid into the chair with her back facing the door. "It's going to be so good to see Cade."

Brooke nodded. "But that's not what I want to talk about. How are you doing?" She knew about the negative pregnancy tests Jen had taken the month before and how disappointed she'd been.

Jen sighed. "I'm fine. My period finally started today, an entire month late. That used to happen before I went on the pill in college. But since then, I've never missed an entire month, except for last summer when I stopped taking the pill. I don't get it."

"I've had that happen once or twice. It's odd for sure. How's Rob?"

"That's what I feel the worst about. He's spent so much time comforting me, and I know he's suffering too. I have an appointment in two weeks, so I'm hoping for some answers." She took a drink of her wine. "You know, if we have to do in vitro, then we're ready to."

Brooke took her hand. "Good. I wondered—" Her eyes went to the door, and her face broke into a huge smile. "Oh my God!"

Jen turned to see what she was looking at and saw Caden walking in with his hand tightly entwined in Quinn's. Both women stood, regarding the couple with grins.

When Caden and Quinn reached the table, Jen put her arms out to hug Quinn. "It's so good to see you!"

Quinn returned her hug with her warm brown eyes shining. "It's good to be here." They separated, and Quinn opened her arms to Brooke. "Hi, Mama."

Brooke whispered as they hugged, "I haven't seen Caden look this happy since February."

Quinn responded, "We're both pretty happy."

Before they could sit, Rob and Danny walked through the door, both smiling when they saw Quinn. Rob reached to hug her, but glanced at Caden first.

Caden smiled and nodded imperceptibly.

Rob wrapped his arms around her and said, "You're looking good, darlin'," then let her go so Danny could move into his space.

Rob reached his hand out to fist-bump Caden, but drew him into a hug instead. As the others were chattering, he said softly to Caden, "Glad we didn't have to use that will."

Caden nodded. "Me too."

Danny said, "This calls for a shot." He went to the bar and returned with a shot of Jameson for everyone but Brooke. "Sorry, babe. Two more months. Cheers to the best reunion we've had in a long while!" They touched their glasses together. "Okay, so tell us all how this came about." He waved his hand between Quinn and Caden.

Caden spoke first. "Well, you know we ended up at the same mission. I'm still not sure that wasn't something Brooke and Claire cooked up, although Quinn insists it wasn't."

"I keep telling you, I wouldn't have been puking in a garbage can that first day if I'd known I was going to see you."

Brooke smiled with delight. "So, once you saw her, you came to your senses, and you've been together since then?"

"Not exactly."

"He totally ignored me the first week, working as far away from me as possible."

Caden took Quinn's hand. "No, it was you staying away from me."

"I'm just a lowly nurse. I went where they told me to go. You could pick where you worked." She looked conspiratorially at Brooke and Jen. "But he sneaked glances at me every night. He thought he was being discreet, but I knew."

Caden's face reddened. "Guilty as charged. The second week, we were assigned to work together, and she assisted me in surgery to remove an appendix."

Danny raised his eyebrows in surprise. "Surgery? You still remember how to do that? It's been a while."

"It's a straightforward procedure. Quinn did great as my nurse."

"Yeah, and my hands were shaking the entire time. You forgot to mention how we were thrown together when one of the nurses fell off the side of the mountain on that hike."

"Yeah. Not my favorite moment." He grimaced. "You all know how I feel about heights."

Jen asked, "So then, did you realize you're meant for each other?"

Quinn looked at Caden, and he nodded, so she responded, "Not exactly, but we started talking to each other. There was a lot to talk about."

When she paused, Caden took up the strand. "A week ago, we were the last ones in the clinic when a young boy with a gunshot wound was brought in. It was some kind of family dispute, and while we were working on him, another car tore onto the property. Both men had firearms, and the first one grabbed Quinn. He shoved a pistol into her back."

Jen and Brooke both gasped.

"Yeah, that gave me instant clarity. I knew at that moment how much I loved her and that I didn't want to spend another second away from her." His grip on Quinn's hand tightened, and he leaned over to kiss her. "And thankfully, she feels the same."

Brooke and Jen smiled through their tears at Caden's declaration.

Danny said, "So, Quinn, when are you moving to Boston? Because you know you'll never get him out of the city."

Caden answered, "Actually, I really enjoyed being in a different environment, so where we're going to live is under discussion. We've done some tweaking to our schedules, and we'll be spending time in both places."

Quinn added, "There's a new exchange program between the two hospitals, and I'm going to work at Mass General for October and November. Then Cade will come to Dartmouth for February and March. We'll decide where we want to be after that."

Danny shook his head. "You're not leaving Boston. I'll never believe that."

Rob said, "Jenny and I spent a week at a cottage on Lake Winnipesaukee in July, and we loved it. I can see why you'd want to move up there."

Quinn clapped her hands. "That's such a beautiful area. Sam and I went camping there after I graduated from high school. Hanover's not quite the same, but it's nice. We're taking our time."

Jen looked at Caden for a reaction to her mention of Sam but didn't see one.

Instead, Caden asked, "So, what's going on with all of you? Brooke, two more months? Everything's all good?"

She nodded in response.

Then he looked at Danny. "How's the job? Any better?"

Danny took a long swallow of his beer and shook his head. "The second lead quit two weeks ago. Which means I get more work dumped on me by the asshole at lead."

Brooke added, "It's been a rough summer."

"Any chance the team will dump him?"

"And give me the job that should have been mine last spring? I doubt it. We're in the middle of preseason. The focus is on the football players now, not media. Let's throw some darts."

When they left, Quinn said, "I didn't realize how bitter he was. And I don't think Caden did either."

Brooke nodded. "Caden isolated himself until just before he left, so he didn't see all of it."

"He told me that. Do you think Caden being back will help?"

Brooke shrugged. "I'll be honest. I don't know how it's going to be when the baby comes. He's so unhappy, and the team's not expected to do well this season either."

"Are you still working?"

"Yes, I've got a couple of jobs to finish before she arrives and some new projects I'm starting next month. I'm going to cut back after the baby comes until the season ends, but I'll have work I can do at home. Danny travels so much with the team that it'll be easier if I don't have any outside commitments."

Quinn looked at Jen. "And what's up with you and Rob?"

"We're still not expecting. I've got an appointment after Labor Day to find out why."

"Cade told me you weren't pregnant when he left. We were hoping something had happened since then. There's so much that can be done. You'll find the answers."

"We'll see. You're going to split your time between Boston and Hanover?"

"Yes, we'll both work some nights, and one or the other of us will travel. We won't be together every night, but it won't just be weekends either. And I can't wait to be here for two months!"

Brooke added, "He's really thinking about moving to Hanover permanently?"

"We've talked about it. He said the solitude and the stars were good for him. It's early. Time will tell. We've talked about everything over the last few weeks, and especially since last week."

"Just talking? Nothing else?" Jen grinned and raised her eyebrows at Quinn.

Quinn blushed under her tan. "Oh, there's been a significant amount of sex too."

As Danny was lining up his dart, Rob asked Caden, "My hugging Quinn wasn't a problem?"

"It wasn't. All that therapy finally kicked in. For a couple of nights in Honduras, we had music, and she danced with some of the other doctors and nurses. It was before the incident with the gun, and we weren't really back together, but it didn't bother me." He threw a dart and hit the bull's-eye. "And if something causes a reaction, we'll handle it together."

"Did you tell her about your will?"

"No," he said, laughing. "She suggested I give all the money away, since it's making me so miserable. We're talking about starting a foundation to support doctors and nurses who want to do humanitarian work." The game finished, and Caden said, "I missed you guys a lot."

Chapter Nine

We've Been Trying For a Year

Robbie

ROBBIE TOOK THE ELEVATOR to the fifth floor and strode down the hall before stopping in front of the desk of Jenny's current intern. "Is she in?" He'd come directly from the courthouse. He wore a dark suit with a white shirt and a blue striped tie. Jenny had told him a day or two before that she thought the intern was crushing on him. Mindful of that, he didn't speak to her in the same flirty way he had used with Jenny's assistant, who had recently retired.

With stars in her eyes, the intern said, "She isn't back from the budget meeting. She said you should wait in her office."

He let himself in and wandered over to a bookcase where she had pictures displayed. He smiled when he saw she had added two photos from their week in New Hampshire. Her office reflected the warmth of her personality, with books and pictures and a vase filled with daisies on her desk. She picked up fresh flowers at the beginning of every week. She'd only been in the management position for a year, and he was the only one who knew how hard she had worked for it.

He walked over to the window. Gazing out, he thought about how Jenny deserved to be in a position to effect change, but her favorite part of the job was the time she spent in the shelters she worked with. He glanced at his watch. *I hope she gets here soon. I'm not sure how her gynecologist's office works, but I don't think we should be late.* He'd never been to any of her appointments, and he was as anxious as she was to get some answers.

When he heard the door open, he swung around. Jenny walked in, carrying notebooks and folders. He hurried to take them from her.

"Dump them on the desk. I'll straighten it all out tomorrow. I thought I'd never get out of there." She opened her desk drawer, pulled out a hair tie, put her hair in a high ponytail, and hugged Robbie. "We need to head out."

When they walked past the intern, Jen said, "I'm done for the day. We have an appointment. There's some stuff I need you to research for me. We'll talk in the morning."

The intern nodded and, with the stars still in her eyes, said, "You two are such a gorgeous couple. You should be in a magazine."

Jen was wearing a royal-blue sheath dress that complemented Robbie's tie. He flashed a smile, and Jen winked at her as they hurried by.

"You didn't call her *darlin'*, did you? She'd melt into a puddle of goo if she heard that Southern drawl."

He chuckled as he took her hand. "No. I behaved myself."

She led him into the doctor's office.

"Wow, we're here already?"

"The closeness is one reason I go here."

She signed in, and they found a place to sit.

Robbie looked around at the women in various stages of pregnancy. Some were alone, and some had a companion with them. *I'll make it to every appointment with Jenny if we ever get to that point.*

A nurse escorted them to an exam room, and Jenny introduced her to Robbie before her vital signs were taken. The doctor came in a few minutes later, and Jenny also introduced her.

She started the conversation by asking what had happened since she had seen Jen in May.

Robbie listened as Jenny described her period being late while they were on vacation. *Late doesn't even describe it. She skipped the entire month.* He remembered the feeling of excitement when they thought she might be pregnant and the crushing disappointment when the three tests she took all came back negative.

The doctor typed as Jen spoke, and when she paused, the doctor said, "This is how I'd like to proceed. The blood tests we conducted in May showed that all your hormone levels were within normal range. There are the fibroids we saw on the ultrasound, but as I told you, I don't believe they're keeping you from conceiving. Before we go into more invasive testing, I'd like Robbie to have his sperm count checked. Are you okay with that?"

He nodded, bringing his attention back to the present. "Uh, sure? How would that be done? I mean, I guess I can imagine, but... is it done here?"

"No, I'll refer you to a urologist. It's low-tech. You just provide a sample, and it's analyzed." Robbie raised his hand, signaling that she didn't need to say any more, and she smiled before she continued. "If everything is normal there, then we'll discuss the next steps. You should be able to get the test done quickly, so we'll schedule your next appointment for two weeks from today."

She paused as she resumed typing. When she finished, she stood, and they followed suit. "We will sort this out, and I'll be with you throughout the journey." She looked directly at Robbie. "The doctor's office will call you with an appointment. You'll need to refrain from ejaculating for three to five days before providing the sample."

They rode the elevator to the ground floor in silence, and when they got outside, Jenny asked, "Are you okay with doing this?"

He scoffed. "Of course. No big deal, and it's easier than some of what you will have to go through." He took her hand. "She seems nice, the doctor."

Jenny nodded.

"I've got a surprise for you. We're meeting Caden and Quinn for dinner."

"At O'Malley's?"

"No, I thought something a little more upscale would be nice." He named a restaurant they both liked on Newbury Street.

They arrived first and settled at the table set with a white tablecloth, heavy silverware, and fall flowers. The dark-colored walls glowed in the late-afternoon sunlight pouring in through the windows.

"Are we celebrating something?"

"Getting started, Caden being back, and his reunion with Quinn." A server came to their table, and as he ordered a bottle of wine, Caden and Quinn approached.

Quinn slid into the chair Caden had pulled out for her, saying, "You two look gorgeous! I need to up my wardrobe if I'm going to be spending more time here. People don't dress like this in rural New Hampshire." She was wearing a simple black dress, and a star, studded with diamonds, hung from a gold chain around her neck.

Jen reached out to touch the star. "That is beautiful!"

Blushing, Quinn said, "Cade bought it for me last weekend. The stars were kind of important to him in Honduras."

He swung his arm over the back of her chair. "Never seen them shine so brightly."

Rob said, "Tell us about the mission. When we got together a couple of weeks ago, you only talked about how the two of you came together. What was it like working there?"

"Intense poverty." Caden glanced at Jen. "I know you see poverty and need every day, as do I, but this was far beyond that. Yet the people were kind and proud. We agree that we'll go back."

Rob said, "I'd like to do that someday. There must be needs beyond medical."

Quinn answered, "There are tons of ways to contribute. You'd both be valuable to the community."

"You really want to start a foundation?"

"I really do. We're going to need legal counsel."

Rob laughed. "Another area of the law outside my field of expertise."

Quinn cocked her head. "Another? Have you done legal work for Caden?"

"You haven't told her?"

Caden shook his head.

"Told me what?" Quinn looked between the two men.

"I changed my will before I left for Honduras. Rob helped me find someone at his firm to do it for me."

"Oh, did you add Rory to it?" They had both fallen in love with his nephew right after he was born. She picked up a roll and started buttering it. "God, I don't even have a will. I've got more debts than assets." She laughed.

Caden took a drink of his wine and stared at the glass, avoiding her gaze.

Rob said, "You need to tell her."

Quinn's eyes shifted between the two men again before she looked at Jen. "Do you know what they're talking about?"

With Caden's permission, Robbie had told her, so she nodded with a look of chagrin.

Caden put the wineglass down and turned to Quinn. "Before I left, I changed my will to name you as the beneficiary."

Quinn blinked twice and looked at the three people at the table. "You did *what*?"

"If something happens to me, everything I have will go to you."

She sat back in her chair, her shock apparent.

"I never stopped loving you, Quinn. Or wanting to take care of you."

When she continued to sit in stunned silence, Caden asked, "Are you still sure I should give all the money away?"

"Yes!" Quinn drummed her fingers on the table. "I can't believe you did that."

Robbie's phone rang, and he pulled it out of his pocket, standing when he saw who was calling. "I need to take this," he said as he walked toward the door.

He came back quickly and said to Jenny, "I've got an appointment tomorrow at ten."

Quinn and Caden were whispering to each other. "Are you angry?"

"No, just shocked!"

"I'm going to take care of all your debts before we start the foundation."

Her eyes widened, and she shook her head. "No, you're not!"

He nodded with a smile on his face.

Finally, Caden and Quinn pulled their attention away from each other and looked at Rob expectantly.

"Our OB-GYN recommended that I have my sperm levels checked. I have an appointment with a urologist tomorrow."

Quinn said, "That's a good first step. Easy, noninvasive."

"I can't go with you tomorrow. I've got more budget meetings." They had agreed to attend all appointments together, and

Robbie had let his office know that his schedule might be erratic for a while. "This happened more quickly than I expected."

"I'll be okay, darlin'. Been going to the doctor by myself for years." When their meal was finished, they lingered at the table. They all ordered coffee, and Rob stretched his long legs out. "Do you two want to go to a Sox game with us this weekend? Friday, Saturday, Sunday, or even all three days?"

Caden raised his eyebrows. "All three days? Against the Yankees? How'd you score those tickets?"

"After we went to that game back in May, I bought season tickets. I discovered that seeing the ballplayers in their baseball pants is an aphrodisiac for Jenny."

Caden burst out laughing, and Quinn looked at Jen, who was blushing.

"Come to the game with us. You'll see. You won't be able to keep your hands off Cade afterward."

Caden wrapped his arms around Quinn. "I like the sound of that. Do you have four?"

Rob nodded. "Danny and Brooke have come with us. He brought Liam to one game, and Jenny's family came to town in August. If there's no one I want to bring, I can always find someone in my office to buy them. Let me know which games work for you."

Chapter Ten

Robbie's Appointment

Robbie

ROB LEFT WORK TO walk to the urologist's office. He was in a good mood as he thought about their dinner the night before. Danny and Caden had been friends almost since they were born, and he was a latecomer to the group, sometimes feeling like a third wheel. Cade's parents had taken him in when his family left Boston, and their bond had grown stronger, but nothing like it had been since Caden started dating Quinn.

He'd worked to maintain contact with Cade after he broke up with Quinn, even when Caden didn't want to see any of them. His actions before he left for Honduras—asking for help with his will and finally opening up about what precipitated the split—made Rob feel appreciated. Danny had been a mess since spring when he didn't get the lead job in the media department, and Rob was wondering when he'd get himself back together. *Maybe when the baby is born.*

His thoughts drifted to his appointment. He and Jenny had googled everything they could find on infertility, so he thought he knew what to expect. He wished she were with him, although the appointment he'd gone to the previous day was the first he'd ever attended with her in all their years together. *I can't believe I'm the problem, but I'll take one for the team.*

After he signed in, he sat down with the voluminous questionnaire the receptionist had given him. He paused when he got to the childhood diseases. *God, there are so many.* He had finally put his pen down when he heard, "Mr. Hatch?"

Rob jumped up, startled and nervous. "I'm right here. That's me."

In the exam room, the nurse recorded his weight and height and took his blood pressure then reached for a small cup. *Man, that was fast. I thought I'd talk to the doctor first, and I was hoping to do it at home with Jenny.*

"Do you think you can give me a sample? The bathroom is right there." She motioned toward another door in the room. "I'll wait here, and you can leave it on the counter when you're done."

Rob's face reddened. "I-I thought it would be a little more private."

"Private? Ohhh." She smiled. "I need a urine sample. Can you do that for me? The semen sample will be later."

He laughed in embarrassment. "You had me in a bit of a panic, darlin'."

She handed him the cup and pointed at the bathroom.

He followed the directions for collecting a clean sample. *I've been lucky. I've been healthy and can't remember having to do this.* He remembered Jenny talking about giving a sample when she had a UTI. When he returned to the exam room, the nurse motioned him to a chair and started going over the questionnaire with him. He felt like every area of his life was under a microscope. She finished, and, as she walked out the door, told him that the doctor would be in soon.

He looked around the office, which featured anatomical posters of the kidneys, bladder, and urinary tract. He pinched the bridge of his nose. *I liked Jenny's doctor's office better. All those warm posters about tiny humans, mothers, and families. This is totally clinical.* He was nervous and hoped the doctor would come in soon. Stretching his legs, he closed his eyes and breathed deeply. The creak of the door opening startled him, and he jumped up much as he had in the waiting room.

"Mr. Hatch? I'm Dr. Nelson." The doctor extended his hand and, after they shook, motioned for Rob to sit down. He opened his laptop and studied it for several minutes before he said anything. "You and your wife have been having unprotected intercourse for a year with no pregnancy resulting?"

"Yes. Actually, a little longer than a year. She stopped taking the pill a year ago in July."

"Any problems in the bedroom? Premature ejaculation? Impotence?"

"No!"

The doctor snapped his eyes up from the keyboard at the indignation in Rob's tone. He raised his hands in surrender. "I have to ask. It's a routine question." He rolled his chair back from the desk and assumed a more casual pose. "This is how we're going to proceed. Now that I've had some time to look over your history, we'll chat for a bit. I have a few questions, then I'll do a physical exam. I'm going to order some labs, and of course, I'll need a semen sample. You can do it here, or some men prefer to do it at home. That works as long as you aren't some long-ass commute away."

Rob laughed nervously. "I live here in the city."

"Good." He looked back at his laptop. "You had more childhood diseases than I typically see in someone your age. Do you remember much about those?"

He shrugged. "There were a lot of us. When one got sick, we all did."

"Two sisters and three brothers. Younger? Older? Do they have children?"

"I'm the oldest, and they all have children."

"Did any of them have difficulty conceiving?"

"We're not close, emotionally or physically. They all live on the West Coast, and I know little about their lives except that we get a birth announcement every time one of them has a baby."

The doctor looked at him for several moments before he said, "On paper, you're in great shape. Perfect weight for your height, you get regular exercise, don't smoke or do drugs, and you don't drink to excess. Let's do the physical exam." He pointed at the exam table. "There's a gown. You should take everything off and put that on. I'll step out to give you some privacy and be back in a couple of minutes."

The exam started at his head and worked its way down. Dr. Nelson spent long enough manipulating his testicles and penis that Rob thought he'd found something wrong. When he finished, he left again so that Rob could dress. He came back in and said, "Everything feels completely normal." Rob blew out the breath he didn't know he'd been holding, and the doctor smiled. "Everyone reacts like that. Here's the cup for your sample. Any idea when you'll bring it in?"

"Tomorrow."

The doctor raised his eyebrows. "It needs to be two to five days since you last ejaculated. I prefer three. Do you fit that window?"

"As it happens, it's been exactly three days since we had intercourse. And we're eager to figure out what the problem is."

"I understand. If we have it tomorrow, I'll probably have the results for you by the beginning of the week. Stop by the lab and have your blood drawn too." He shook Rob's hand. "It was a pleasure meeting you. I hope I can help you get some answers."

As Rob walked back to his office, he took his phone out to let Jenny know he was done. *God, I was in there for over two hours. I'm exhausted.*

Robbie pulled the covers over his head, trying to block out the sunlight so he could grab a few more minutes of sleep, but the smell of fresh coffee lured him out. He pushed up to sit and made room for Jenny beside him.

When she handed him a mug, he took a deep swallow. "Ahhh, why can't we start every morning like this?" They had both delayed going to work so that he could provide his sample.

"Because we both have these pesky careers. And we've got a job to get done this morning." She rubbed her hand over his thigh and let it drift up to his crotch.

"Darlin', I just woke up. Give me a minute."

She laughed.

Robbie had never been a fan of early-morning intercourse. After gulping his last swallow of coffee, he went to the bathroom and looked more awake when he returned. He reached for Jenny's mug and placed it on the floor, pulled on the tie of her silky robe, and slid it down over her arms. "I like the way you look in the morning."

"Did you wash up the way the instructions said to?"

Robbie rolled his eyes and huffed. "Yes. I'm sorry. I don't mean to be annoyed. It's just so clinical."

"I know. Let's make it fun." She smashed her lips against his and pinched his nipple.

He wrapped his arms around her and moved his hands up and down her back then let them travel to her butt.

She snaked her hand down to his cock, which had hardened in response to her touch. They separated slightly, and he took one of her breasts in his mouth. Moaning, she increased her pressure on his cock.

He thrust toward her, and she slowed down.

"I want to watch you. I know you thought I'd do it, but..." She flashed the shy smile that made him remember the first time they'd made love.

Rolling away from her, he took his cock in his right hand and started slowly stroking it.

Jenny idly made circles around one of his nipples.

Robbie focused on her face then moved his free hand onto hers, slowing the circles. "Turning you on?" He grinned at her, already knowing the answer.

She nodded.

"You can touch yourself too."

"No, I want to concentrate on you."

Robbie picked up his pace. "Won't have time to take care of you when I finish."

"You could take it to the office and come back. I don't have to be at work until noon."

"Mmmm, I like the way you think." His hand was stroking faster, and his breath was coming quicker. "Close. Really close."

Jenny moved the sample cup into place just as he exploded into it with a groan.

"Oh, man." He stretched out with his heart pounding.

She leaned in to kiss him. "I love you so much."

As his heart rate returned to normal, he pulled her down to him. "I can't linger." He kissed her. "That needs to be at the office within an hour."

She nuzzled his neck and let him get up. "Are you going to come back?"

"Yeah, I'm just going to throw my clothes on, get this over there, and come back to shower and dress for work." When she looked at him expectantly, he smiled. "Maybe I'll find something else to do while I'm here." He pulled his jeans on and tugged a sweatshirt over his head before he picked up the sample. "Don't move. I'll be back as soon as I can."

Chapter Eleven

The Results Are In

Robbie

IT WAS NEARLY THE end of the day on Monday when Robbie made his way from the courthouse to his office. *I could go straight home, but I want to see how things are lining up for tomorrow, and I need to check my messages.* Normally, he checked his messages and emails on his phone, but it had died while he was in court.

His mood was good. The trial he'd been at went his way, and the Sox had taken two out of three games from the Yankees over the weekend. Quinn and Caden had gone to the Friday and Saturday games with them, and they'd taken Liam on Sunday.

Danny was busy with the football game, and Brooke welcomed a chance for a quiet afternoon by herself.

When he reached his office, he plugged in his phone while he booted up his laptop. He ran through his emails and had just finished listening to his office voicemails when his cell phone sprang to life. He scanned text messages from Jenny, Caden, and Danny before looking at the missed calls. *Holy shit, there's a voicemail from the urologist.* He hesitated before he listened to it, nervous to hear the results.

"Hi, Mr. Hatch. This is Dr. Nelson's office. He has your results and would like you to come in to discuss them. His last appointment is at three-thirty, so he can see you at four-thirty or later. Please call and let us know when you'll be here."

Robbie looked at the time. *Four. I can be there by four thirty.* He called to let them know. "Can't you give me the results over the phone?"

"No, Dr. Nelson prefers you come in so he can discuss the results with you. And bring your wife."

Blood rushed to Robbie's face, and his heart started pounding. *I don't like this. Why can't he tell me over the phone?* He called Jenny, but it went to voicemail. "Hey, babe. Dr. Nelson wants me to go to his office to get my results. I told him I'd be there at four thirty. Can you meet me there? Please?"

He walked all the way to the office to burn off the nervous energy coursing through his body. *God, I hope Jenny makes it.*

He arrived with ten minutes to spare, and as he pulled out his phone to call Jenny again, she appeared in front of him.

He reached out his arms to her. "I'm so glad you're here. I'm nervous. Why does he want to see me?"

She smiled and ran her fingers through his hair. "Let's go inside and find out."

The waiting room was empty, and they were escorted immediately to the doctor's office, where they sat, and Robbie bounced his leg nervously.

Jenny took his hand. "Babe, I don't think I've ever seen you like this."

He shook his head and put his other hand on his leg, trying to stop its movement.

The doctor walked in, shook Robbie's hand, and introduced himself to Jenny before he sat down at his desk. He hit a few keys on his laptop and studied the screen for a few minutes. "These are difficult results to convey. Your sperm count is very low. Anything less than fifteen million sperm per milliliter is low, and your count is five million per milliliter." He let what he was telling them sink in.

Robbie stuttered, "Are-Are you sure? I-I-I-I mean, you asked when I had last ejaculated. Could the time have been too short?" He tightened his grip on Jenny's hand.

Dr. Nelson said gently, "It's unlikely unless you gave me incorrect information. You said it had been three days. That's within the timeframe we look for."

"Can... Should we do it again? Could there have been a problem in the lab?"

"We can do that, but it's not only the count. There's also a problem with the motility. That's..."

Robbie snapped at him. "We know what that is. They don't swim like they should."

"Yes. There are some things we can do. Do you want to discuss that now, or do you want some time to absorb this?"

Jenny answered, "We'd like to hear what you recommend."

The doctor covered several procedures and tests and handed her literature about each one. "I know you've done research, but this will give you more information. Take some time to study these and decide how you want to proceed. There are many alternatives available to help you have the children you want."

"Thank you. Robbie, let's get going. We need to take some time to process everything."

They made their way home silently, with their hands clenched tightly together.

When they stepped into their house, Robbie said, "I think I'll go for a run. Do you mind?"

"Of course not. Whatever you need." She put her hand on his cheek. "Robbie, we'll be okay."

He pulled her close and held her silently.

After his run, Jenny opened the door as soon as he stepped onto the porch. It was a warm fall afternoon, and he was dripping with sweat. She held a towel out for him, and he peeled off his T-shirt.

"We need that outdoor shower here," she said.

Robbie smiled wanly as he grabbed the towel. He wiped his torso and rubbed the towel over his hair. "I've got to get in the shower. I'm gross."

"Are you hungry?"

He shrugged and climbed the stairs to the bathroom. When he came back down, dressed in a white T-shirt and navy shorts, he found a platter with cheese, apple slices, and grapes, along with a can of beer. He sank onto the couch and absentmindedly grabbed a slice of cheese. His phone was on the coffee table, and he picked it up, quickly typing in the search bar.

Jenny sat beside him, watching as he concentrated on the screen.

Abruptly, he threw the phone onto the love seat on the other side of the room. "Fuck my fucking family!"

Jenny jumped, unaccustomed to outbursts like that from him. She put her hand on his arm. "Robbie! What's going on?"

He slumped back on the couch, resting his head against the cushion and staring at the ceiling. After a few minutes, he sighed, straightened, and turned toward Jenny. "My parents don't believe in vaccinations. When I met Dr. Nelson last week, he remarked that I'd had more childhood diseases than he usually sees in someone my age. I told him there were a lot of us, and when one got sick, we all did." He took a swallow of his beer. "But the truth is, it was because I hadn't been vaccinated. None of us were. I had chicken pox, rubella, whooping cough, and mumps."

He stopped and clasped her hands. "I'd heard that mumps can cause sterility, but I thought it was an old wives' tale." He shook his head. "Turns out it's not. That's what I was looking up on my phone. Go ahead. Read it."

Jenny retrieved his phone and looked at the screen. "It looks like it's not a sure thing, Robbie. Mumps doesn't necessarily cause sterility."

"But they can. I had them when I was thirteen, and I was extremely sick. And now I find out I'm sterile. It's a logical conclusion. Don't try to convince me not to blame my parents!"

She sat silently for several minutes. "I'm not defending them. You've told me so little."

"I had myself emancipated from my parents and moved in with Caden's family when I was seventeen. Sean, Maureen, and the rest of the Bradys became my family. My father was an authoritarian asshole who told me I'd never see them again if I didn't move with them, and I haven't." He had told her he was estranged from his family, and she hadn't pushed for more. "I can't believe they're still affecting my life after all these years." His voice broke, and he wrapped his arms around her.

Holding him, she rubbed her hands up and down his back. "It's okay. We'll be okay."

Robbie pulled back from her, his face a picture of devastation. "I'm so sorry, babe. It's *my* fault! We've talked about what our kids would be like since that first summer. And I'm the reason we don't have them." He struggled to hold back tears.

"Dr. Nelson gave me several brochures. There are a lot of things we can try. Do you want to look at them tonight?"

Robbie took in her expectant gaze. *It's the last thing I want to do, but I know she wants to.* "Sure. You probably have them all memorized, don't you?"

She grinned. "Not memorized, but I have some thoughts. We can try intrauterine insemination. Of course, it has an acronym, IUI. We could do it relatively soon." She handed him a brochure.

Robbie read it. "The sperm gets 'washed' before you're inseminated." He tossed the brochure onto the coffee table and leaned back, staring at the ceiling again.

Jenny sat silently for a few minutes. "Tell me what you're thinking. Please."

"We're doing a science experiment. It's not how I pictured making a baby."

"What matters is that we have a child at the end of it."

"I know." He leaned forward, resting his elbows on his knees. "I'm not in the right headspace to talk about this tonight. Can we just go to bed?"

"We haven't really had dinner."

"Fruit and cheese. I'm not hungry, babe."

Jenny frowned. "Why don't you go upstairs, then? I'll be up in a little bit."

Jenny

Jen took the tray back to the kitchen and stood at the counter, eating the cheese and fruit. *This was the last thing I expected. He'll be okay. He just needs a little time to let it sink in.* After tidying the kitchen, she went upstairs, where Robbie was stretched on the bed with his eyes closed, though she didn't think he was asleep. She changed into a tank top and shorts before crawling under the covers next to him.

On a normal night, even if they didn't make love, they spent time wrapped in each other's arms, but Robbie made no movement toward her. She flipped the light switch and lay silently on her back in the dark.

"I'm sorry, babe. I don't mean to be a jerk. It's... It's a lot to take in."

"I know. But we'll get through it."

"I'm going to Cade's tomorrow night to work out. I'm going to tell him. Is that okay?"

"Of course."

"Are you going to tell Brooke?"

"Would you mind?"

"No." Jenny could hear the hesitation in his voice.

"I'm not planning to call her and make a big announcement, but she knows we've had some appointments. It'll come up the next time we're together." She sighed. "You don't want me to, do you? Because of Danny?"

"He'll probably be a jerk." Robbie huffed out a breath. "He's changed so much."

"I'll tell Brooke my doctor has more tests she wants to do. I won't do anything that makes you uncomfortable."

He took a deep breath and reached for Jenny's hand. "The insemination would happen when you're ovulating?"

"Yes."

"And you're already tracking that, so we're halfway there. Where are you in your cycle?"

"My period's just finishing, so I'll ovulate in a couple of weeks."

"Think we can do it then?"

"Maybe. Let's talk more tomorrow."

Robbie rolled toward Jenny, and she put her arms around him, pulling him close and settling his head on her shoulder.

Chapter Twelve

Sharing The Burden

Robbie

"ALL THAT MONEY I spent on condoms when we were in high school..." Rob had just climbed off the slant board and swallowed a sip of water before continuing. "Turns out it was wasted."

Caden had a fifteen-pound weight in each hand and stopped mid-curl. "What are you saying?" His eyes narrowed.

"My sperm count... My sperm count is low." He took a deep breath. "For all intents and purposes, I'm sterile." He sat down. "We found out yesterday."

"Oh man. That's a blow."

Rob nodded. "It sure was."

"I'm truly sorry. I know how much you and Jen want a baby."
He hesitated. "Not to sound like a cliché, but there are other
ways."

"Oh yeah, we came home with a fistful of brochures outlin-
ing the alternatives."

Caden tossed a towel to Rob and ran another one over his
torso. "I don't mean to go all medical on you if what you're
looking for is just a friendly ear, but how low are you talking?
Nonexistent or just lower than normal?"

"Five million per milliliter." Rob could read the expression
on Caden's face. "You don't even need to say anything."

"It's not my area of expertise. You know that. But yeah, that's
low."

"And there are motility issues."

"Fuck, a double whammy."

Rob nodded.

"This is what we're going to do. Sit in the sauna for ten
minutes. You can shower here, then we're going to go up to my
den and have a shot of Irish whiskey."

Twenty minutes later, Rob settled on the leather sofa in Caden's den. While Caden poured the shots, he sent a text to Jenny.

> *Having a shot with Cade. Home in
> forty-five minutes.*

Rob took the shot from Caden and gazed at the fire.

"How's Jen taking this?"

"You know her." Rob switched his gaze from the fireplace to Caden. "Ever the optimist. She wanted to discuss it last night, and I'm sure she has our next five moves planned. I know it was wrong, but I just couldn't talk about it. I needed time to let it sink in."

Caden nodded. One thing Rob liked about Caden was that he knew when to be quiet. And this was one of those times.

"She mentioned doing IUI. You know what that is?"

Caden nodded again.

"I reacted kind of badly to that. Told her it sounds like a science experiment." Rob shook his head. "Classy, huh?"

"We all have our moments."

"Yeah. So we'll try that, hopefully in a couple of weeks. If that doesn't work, I think IVF will be the next step."

"If you need assistance, financially speaking, you know I'm happy to help. My grandfather would be thrilled to think his money went to help you have a baby."

"I knew you'd say that, but we should be fine. God, I wish Paddy had met Jenny. Wouldn't he have loved her?"

"He would have. And I've been thinking about how much he would have loved Quinn." Caden poured another shot for each of them.

Rob raised his glass toward Caden, who tapped his glass against it. "To Paddy."

Caden nodded with a smile. "To Paddy." Then he downed the shot.

Quinn appeared in the doorway. "What's the occasion calling for shots on a weeknight?" She crossed the room and sat on the arm of Caden's chair, leaning in to kiss him.

"How was your drive?" he murmured.

Quinn had driven to Boston after working her shift at Dartmouth. "It was good. Leaving an hour later lets me miss rush hour. Now I'm looking forward to three days with you."

"Hey, Quinn." *I'm going to tell her. It's nothing to be ashamed of, and this is a safe space to get used to saying the words.* "Remember that appointment I had with a urologist last week?"

When she nodded, he continued, "It turns out my sperm count is very low. I'm functionally sterile." His voice cracked on the last word.

"Oh, Rob. I'm so sorry."

What's the proper response? "Thanks. We found out yesterday."

"I imagine you're still digesting the news."

He shrugged.

"Were you offered alternatives? There are other ways to make a baby." She grinned. "Not as much fun, but you get what you want in the end."

"Yeah, we came home with all kinds of information."

"I'm going to leave you guys alone." She kissed Caden then walked over to Rob and leaned down to hug him. She whispered, "You two will be okay."

"Thanks." Rob ran a hand through his hair.

Before leaving the study, Quinn stopped. "Would it be okay if I reached out to Jen? Maybe tomorrow? Or would she rather not talk about it?"

"I think she'll be happy to hear from you."

Quinn nodded. "I'm rooting for you."

After Quinn had walked away, Rob asked, "When are you going to propose?"

"Soon."

"Really? I was just playing with you. Didn't expect that answer."

Caden walked to the bar. "One more?"

Rob held out his glass.

After taking a swallow, Caden said, "I'm working on a plan. But I can tell you this. It won't be a long engagement."

"Big fancy wedding?"

"Whatever Quinn wants, but honestly, I hope not. I'd go to city hall the day after I proposed."

Rob sent Jenny another text.

> *One morphed into three. Calling an Uber now.*

Walking Rob to the door, Caden said, "Quinn spoke for me too. We're both rooting for you."

Jenny

Jenny was curled up on the sofa watching the Red Sox game when Robbie walked in. She had on one of his old jerseys from Boston University and a pair of shorts. A glass of wine was sitting on the coffee table beside the brochures they'd been given the day before.

Robbie sat next to her and rubbed his jaw. "You've been crying. I didn't mean to be so late."

"It's okay. I'm enjoying my date with the boys of summer in their tight pants."

"I should have been here. Should have skipped the workout."

She took his hands. "Robbie, you needed to talk to Cade. It's fine. The feelings overwhelmed me for a few minutes. The tears flowed, and I feel better now. But I'm worried about you. It's a lot to take in."

"It is. To tell the truth, not much lawyer work was done in my office today. I spent most of the day online, reading about male infertility, and I learned a lot. Including the fact that the way I'm feeling is not unusual." He wrapped his arm around her back. "We should do the IUI like we talked about last night. And let's do it as soon as possible. Maybe my little tadpoles aren't as bad as we're thinking."

"I'll call in the morning to see what we have to do to get things rolling." She finished her wine. "Let's go to bed."

When they reached the bedroom, Jenny crawled under the covers and watched Robbie undress. *He has the best body. I can't believe it's letting him down this way.*

"Rob was talking to Cade when I arrived last night, and he told me about the test results."

Jen and Quinn were having lunch at a café near Jen's office.

"He needed to talk to someone, and Cade's a good sounding board. I'm sorry he took away some of the precious time you have with Caden."

Quinn waved her hand, dismissing Jen's concerns. "Caden has a time deficit going on with his friends. He told me how he withdrew from them after he broke it off with me. When you add that to the time he spent in Honduras, it amounts to a huge lack. I don't want to take him away from his friends."

"It was almost two months before he went back to O'Malley's on Friday night. Robbie reached out repeatedly, but Cade didn't respond. It's the longest they've gone without getting together." Jen paused. "Robbie was a little lost. You heard how Danny fell apart when he didn't get the promotion?"

Quinn nodded.

"He started drinking. A lot. Robbie said O'Malley's wasn't the same when every Friday night involved babysitting Danny."

"I got the impression the situation hasn't improved."

"It hasn't." Jen shook her head. "Brooke's concerned about what's going to happen when the baby is born."

"That's understandable." Quinn paused. "It's been a rough year."

"Maybe you and Cade working things out will be the start of a change."

"I hope so." Quinn placed her hand on top of Jen's. "I'm so sorry about Rob's results."

"It was a shock. We never expected that." She looked away from the table before turning back to Quinn. "I've never seen Robbie upset in that way. And I don't know how to comfort him."

"Did the doctor give you alternatives? There are things you can try."

"He did. We came home with all kinds of information, but that first night, Robbie didn't want to talk about any of it. He said we'll be doing a science experiment."

Quinn winced.

"I know. That hurt. I went into problem-solving mode, and he withdrew. I have to tamp down my enthusiasm. My natural tendency is to charge in and try everything."

"I'd probably want to do that too."

"Last night, Robbie was in a better frame of mind when he came home. We have an appointment on Friday with a fertility specialist. I'm hoping we can try IUI the next time I'm ovulating."

"Will you try IVF?"

"Oh yeah, we've already talked about that. But there's a lot to that. I'm really hoping the IUI will work."

"I hope so for you."

They both ordered apple crisp for dessert.

"Let's talk about you," Jen said. "Not long until you move in with Cade for two months."

Quinn's face blossomed into a smile. "Yes. I can't wait." Her smile faded slightly. "Cade asked me to move in with him when we were on our way home from Honduras. The hardest thing I ever did was saying no to that. I wasn't ready to give up my job and my life in Hanover. Just like I don't want him to give up Friday nights with Rob and Danny. This is the perfect compromise."

"We're all going to have so much fun. Boston is amazing in the fall. I'm so glad you'll be here."

Chapter Thirteen

Jenny Is Not Fine

Robbie

"Hey, darlin'."

Jenny was waiting on the sidewalk when Robbie walked out of his office. He embraced her briefly and kissed her cheek.

"It's about two blocks from here. I'm glad we could get in so quickly."

"Me too." She slid her arm around Robbie's waist, and he slung his arm over her shoulders to pull her close. "I had a choice, and Dr. Lynch could get us in sooner." She had told him when and where the appointment was, but he hadn't asked her any questions. Conversation between them had been strained since Monday.

"I'm sorry I didn't ask you more about it." He shook his head. "I'm still having a hard time processing this."

"I know. I'm trying to give you space. But, babe. Let me help. Please."

Robbie stopped walking and gathered her into a genuine hug. "I'll try to do better. It'll be good to take some action. I can't wait to do the IUI. You'll ovulate next week?"

Jenny nodded.

"Maybe you'll be pregnant by the first of October."

A nurse escorted them into the exam room, collected their paperwork, and left, telling them the doctor would be right in.

Half an hour later, they were still waiting.

Robbie sank into his thoughts, not saying a word to Jenny. He stood and walked to the small window. After a few minutes, he turned to face her. Tapping his chin, he said, "I've never waited this long in a doctor's office. Have you?" His frustration was obvious.

Jenny shook her head.

"This is ridiculous."

Robbie paced the length of the office then slumped back into his chair just before the doctor entered. He stood to greet him, extending his hand, which the doctor barely touched before sitting behind his desk.

Dr. Lynch picked up the paperwork and studied it, flipping through the pages. Finally, he put the file down. "I can refer you to a sperm bank. That will be your first step."

"A *sperm bank*?" Robbie exclaimed.

Jenny grasped his arm. "We were hoping to try IUI with Robbie's sperm. I'll be ovulating at the end of next week."

"You don't just walk in and ask for IUI to be done. You both need to have a comprehensive fertility workup. We do a detailed semen analysis and check your ovarian reserves, hormone levels, and whether your fallopian tubes are open. Depending on availability, possibly, we'll have the results and be able to do the procedure when you ovulate next month." He picked up the papers, ran his finger along one of the sheets, then dropped them on his desk and looked at Jenny. "You won't get pregnant with this sperm count. As I said at the beginning, I can refer you to a sperm bank."

Robbie stood. "Let's go."

Jenny grabbed his hand. "Robbie..."

Dr. Lynch spoke at the same time. "I know it's hard to hear, but you need to be realistic."

Robbie ignored him. "We're done here, Jenny. Let's go."

Back on the sidewalk, he exploded. "Jesus, he's more than half an hour late, doesn't apologize, then calls me useless!" Trembling with anger, Robbie strode toward the subway, leaving Jenny to catch up with him. He reached the T stop and leaned against the wall.

Jenny looked at him with fire in her eyes. "That was rude. I've never seen you be rude like that."

"Fuck, Jenny. How did you want me to act?" He rubbed his hand over his jaw. "He was rude to us. We will not work with someone who treats us like that." Robbie walked down the stairs to the train.

They stood in silence until Jenny asked, "What do you want to do now?"

Robbie shook his head. "I don't know."

In silence, they rode to their stop.

As he walked in the door of their house, he ripped off his tie. "I'm going for a run."

"Fine," Jenny's tone told him nothing was fine. "I'm meeting Brooke and Quinn for dinner." Then she walked out.

Robbie changed into his running clothes and sent Caden a text letting him know he'd be late getting to O' Malley's. He sat on the bed to put on his sneakers and rubbed his forehead. Then he picked up his phone and sent Jenny a text.

> I'm not telling Danny about my test results. I don't have it in me to listen to his shit. Provided you haven't already told Brooke, do you think you could refrain from telling her?

Her response came back quickly.

> Fine.

114

He ran his usual six-mile route with the doctor's words pounding in his head. "You won't get pregnant with this sperm count. You won't get pregnant with this sperm count." He couldn't escape it. Back at the house, he leaned his head against the shower glass and let the hot water beat on him. *Jenny's pissed. How do I make this right? There must be other specialists we can work with.*

"It's about time you got here. That making-babies excuse is getting old." Danny was already several beers in when Rob arrived at O'Malley's.

The words hurt, but Rob pretended to let them wash over him. The old Danny would have been understanding. He might have razzed Rob a little, but he would have known when to stop. It was hard to know which version of Danny was drinking with them that night. "I'm here now." Rob ordered a beer and chased it with a shot of Jameson. He felt the tension ease for the first time since Monday, and he ordered another one.

"Are we celebrating?" Danny ordered shots for himself and Caden. "Have you finally knocked up your wife?"

"Just happy it's Friday night."

Caden remained silent, watching the baseball game on the monitor over the bar. When Danny went to the restroom, Caden said, "You're going to have to tell him at some point."

"Not with the way he's been since he didn't get the promotion. Any empathy he used to have has gone out the window."

Rob swallowed another shot. "I know it makes things difficult for you, and I'll tell him eventually. But not tonight."

"How'd the appointment go?"

Rob looked at the floor. "Great. It's fun hearing your wife get told she won't get pregnant with your sperm." He relayed the story of what had happened in Dr. Lynch's office and how they had left. "I can't picture you ever being an ass like that with a patient."

"I hope I'm not. Doctors have bad days. Maybe you caught him on one of his. You said he was late. Who knows what had delayed him."

"Don't make me think I should cut him some slack. I'm enjoying my righteous anger."

Danny returned, cutting off their conversation, and the rest of the evening was spent watching the Red Sox and discussing their chances in the playoffs.

As Rob went to the restroom before they left the bar, he heard Danny talking to Caden. "He's had more than me tonight."

"Looks that way. I'm going to have to make sure both of you get home okay."

The three of them walked out the door, and Rob staggered toward the T stop. Caden grabbed the back of his shirt. "Hold up, cowboy. I've called a rideshare."

Rob stumbled up the stairs to his house, aware of Caden watching from the car. Opening the door, he waved to let Caden know he was okay. He carefully made his way through the darkened house, stripping off his clothes when he reached the bedroom. Jenny was lying on her back, and Robbie crawled under the sheets next to her. When she said nothing, he mumbled, "I'm sorry."

"Is that the alcohol talking?"

"Jenny, I never want to hurt you. You know that."

"Well, you did. You embarrassed me at Dr. Lynch's office, and you shut the door on what could be a path forward. Then you ask me not to tell Brooke what's going on. After you, she's my best friend, and I can't talk to her about what is the biggest challenge I've ever had. You're not talking to me, so who do I have? No one." She punctuated her words by turning away from him.

Robbie awoke to find Jenny still in bed, looking at the ceiling. "You said you had a choice of fertility specialists. Let's try the other one." When she didn't answer, he turned to face her. "I'm sorry I acted like a jerk yesterday. It doesn't mean I don't want us to explore our options." There was still no response. "Jenny, talk to me. Please."

"I'll call on Monday." She turned toward him. "When we saw Dr. Nelson at the beginning of the week, he told us there would be more testing, but you had zoned out. I knew going into Dr. Lynch's that nothing was going to happen quickly, but I couldn't bring myself to tell you that. I don't know how to talk to you." Her eyes drilled into his. "And that's never happened."

"I didn't expect this to hit me so hard. I'll try to do better."

The weekend passed with an uneasy vibe, and Robbie was relieved when one of his guardian ad litem kids asked to meet with him. Normally, he hated being pulled away from Jenny on Saturday, but leaving the house for a couple of hours was a welcome respite.

"I need to pack." Jenny pushed back from the table after dinner on Sunday night.

"Pack?"

"I have those meetings in New York City. My flight is in the morning, and I'll be back on Tuesday night."

"Does that mean you won't be able to call the other specialist?"

"I'm going to my office before I leave, and I'll make the call then."

Chapter Fourteen

Relatable

Robbie

"They can't get us in for six weeks." Jenny's voice sounded pinched over the phone.

"Damn. But you made an appointment, right?"

"Yeah, it's at the end of October. I asked them to put us on a waiting list in case they get a cancellation. My ride to the airport is here. I'll see you tomorrow night." She paused, but before Robbie responded, she added. "I love you."

"You're my whole heart, Jenny." He'd ended every phone call with her that way since shortly after they started dating.

Robbie leaned back in his chair, the file he'd been studying when she called forgotten on his desk. *I have to get myself together. We can't have this tension between us for six weeks.* Secretly, he wondered if the long wait meant it was a better practice than the one they had gone to the week before. *Maybe we aren't the only people Dr. Lynch has been rude to.*

The house echoed with loneliness that night. Both he and Jen traveled for work occasionally, and Robbie hated it when she was gone. He picked up food from a Vietnamese food truck on his way home, and after he ate, he stared at the brochures Dr. Nelson had given them. Jenny's words from Saturday morning echoed in his mind. "You zoned out." She wasn't wrong. He hadn't expected to hear that he was the reason they didn't already have a baby.

Scooping up the brochures, he stretched out on the couch. With the Red Sox game on in the background, he studied the pamphlets with the same intensity he had employed when he was studying for the bar. By the time he went to bed, he had a thorough understanding of what was ahead of them, and he was ready for it.

"I'm looking for Robert Hatch."

"This is Robert." His assistant had put through the call, letting him know the caller had indicated it was personal.

"I'm calling from the practice of Dr. Kerr. This is very last-minute, but we have a cancellation at eleven this morning if you can make it. I tried to call Ms. Hatch, but it went to voicemail. She gave us your number as an alternative."

His mind raced. *Should I go to the appointment without Jenny? If I go by myself, I'll have to be present. I can get my questions answered.* Maybe that was the way to show her he was as invested in the process as she was. "My wife is out of town until tomorrow night. Can I come by myself? We'd really like to get this process started."

"Usually, couples come together, especially for the first visit. May I put you on hold?" She was only off the line for a minute. "Dr. Kerr said that would be fine. We have your records." She gave him the address and ended the call.

They have our records. He took a deep breath. *They know I'm the problem.* "You won't get pregnant with that sperm count." Rob was determined to be a better patient than he had been during the last two visits. He called Jenny, not expecting an answer but hoping she wouldn't be angry—angrier—that he was going to the appointment alone.

"Hey." She answered on the second ring.

Robbie launched into his account of the call from Dr. Kerr's office.

"Are you okay with me going alone? I spent last night reading the brochures Dr. Nelson's office gave us. I want to do better." He held his breath.

"It's fine." Her voice had softened, and *fine* didn't hold the same vitriol it had on Friday. "Once we have that first appointment, we'll be in their queue, and the next ones will be easier to schedule."

"I wondered if it would work that way."

"I can't wait to hear all about it."

Rob sat nervously in the waiting room, startled when a tall, gray-haired man dressed in scrubs approached him.

"Mr. Hatch? Follow me, please."

"Are you a nurse?" Rob knew it was sexist, but he'd expected to have his vitals taken by a female.

"I'm a nurse practitioner." He extended his hand. "Jed Kerr. We're short a nurse today, and since I was going to see you anyway, it makes sense for me to do it all."

Rob sat quietly, keeping his feet flat on the floor, while the blood pressure cuff tightened around his arm. *Nurse practitioner? I thought we were seeing a full-fledged doctor. Is this like seeing a paralegal when you're charged with murder? Jesus, don't be judgmental.*

"You can call me Jed." He tapped on the keyboard then pushed his chair away from the desk. "My wife, Ivy, and I run the practice together. She's the doctor at Dr. Kerr and Associates. We both have extensive training and experience in fertility. She'll come in before you leave, but we thought I might be more relatable for you."

Rob ran a hand through his hair. "Not sure I feel relatable to anyone right now."

"That's understandable. My wife and I couldn't conceive. That's how we ended up specializing in fertility."

I want to ask if he was the problem, but I feel like that's out of bounds.

"I have an extremely low sperm count." He smiled as Rob's eyes widened. "So... relatable."

Rob nodded. "I... I don't even know what to say. Were you surprised?" He ran a hand through his hair again. "I know I'm not here to talk about you, but it was such a shock. It's been a week, and I'm still trying to process it."

"Ivy and I believe in treating the whole patient—mind, body, and soul. It's not unusual to have tears shed in our office. We're not shrinks, and we can make referrals for that if it's needed, but we're good listeners, and that's why you're seeing me first. To answer your question, yes, I was surprised." He hesitated. "Although I shouldn't have been. Ivy has a daughter from a prior relationship, so we knew she could conceive. We tried for over a year then started investigating why nothing was happening."

"Jenny and I have been talking about what our kids would be like since shortly after we started dating. I feel like I'm letting her down."

Jed nodded but said nothing, so Rob continued.

"We saw a specialist on Friday, and I was a jerk. But he was a jerk first." He sighed. "You don't need to be a shrink to tell me that looking for someone to blame is classic avoidance behavior."

"It's good that Ivy and I are the second practitioners you're seeing. You got all that jerky behavior out of the way. Anything else on your mind?"

"I don't have any interest in sex." He felt his face heat. "We have... Or we had a good sex life. And now, what's the point? Jenny wants to do IUI, and I told her it feels like we're doing a science experiment. More of me being a jerk."

"Those are all valid feelings. Let me start by telling you that every test we recommend for you, I had myself. So when I say I know how you feel, I really do."

"That's... comforting." Rob took a deep breath and held it before exhaling. "What's the first step?"

"We'll start with another semen analysis, blood work to test your hormone levels, and a scrotal ultrasound. I also want to do a complete physical. We'll schedule that for next week."

When a soft knock sounded on the door, Jed said, "Come in."

A woman wearing a white coat extended her hand to Rob as soon as she entered. "I'm Ivy Kerr. I hope the two of you have had a chance to get acquainted."

Rob stood and was pleased by her firm grip. "I think we have. I'm sorry my wife isn't able to be here. She's out of town, and we're eager to move forward."

"I completely understand. We should be able to get both of you in next week for complete physicals, and I'll chat with her then. Do you have any questions for me?"

Rob hesitated. "Jed told me you had trouble conceiving. Were you successful eventually? If that's not appropriate to ask, just tell me."

Ivy picked a framed photo off her desk and handed it to him. It showed a woman with a strong resemblance to Ivy holding an infant, with a toddler standing in front of her. Jed and Ivy were in the middle of the picture, and beside them were a young man and woman with brown skin and dark hair. "I had Ellie when I was very young, before I met Jed, and we adopted Luis and Camila from Colombia. Our attempts to conceive were unsuccessful, but I can assure you Luis and Cami are totally our children."

"Jenny is a social worker, and I volunteer as a guardian ad litem. We've always talked about adoption. But we thought we'd give birth to a couple of kids first."

"We will do everything we can to facilitate that, but I'm glad to hear you're open to adoption."

Robbie watched Jenny's eyes widen when she stepped out of the terminal, on her way to a bus that would take her into the city. "I didn't expect to see you here." She stood on her tiptoes to kiss him.

Robbie wrapped his arms around her. "I missed you. The house isn't home when you're not there." He held her for several seconds, taking comfort in the press of her body against him and hoping that they were past the coldness there had been between them for more than a week. He took her tote bag as they walked to the bus.

"I'm excited to hear about the appointment today."

"It was good. Really good. Dr. Kerr's husband is a nurse practitioner. And... he's sterile." He blew out his breath. "That's getting easier for me to say."

Jenny caressed his cheek. "I'm glad."

"I think it will be good working with them. We both have appointments next week."

Later, Robbie was lying face down when Jenny came out of the bathroom. Sitting on the bed beside him, she started rubbing his back. He loved having her hands on his body, and he sighed to signal his enjoyment. Eventually, she pushed the shirt up to his shoulders, and he squirmed out of it.

She reached to the nightstand for a bottle of massage oil, squeezed a small puddle onto his back, and languidly spread it over his skin. As she continued to knead his muscles, she said, "I thought I missed you while I was in New York, but truthfully, I was missing you before I left." She dug into his shoulder blade. "We've never had a week where we've said so little to each other."

Robbie groaned as her fingers plied a knot. He writhed in contentment as the tension left his body. Jenny's hands moved toward his butt, and she leaned forward to flutter a kiss on his neck. He flipped over and gazed at her. "Your hands are magic."

She ran them over his chest. "You're very tense."

"Come here." He circled his arms around her, drawing her to him. When she relaxed against him, more of his tension faded away. His lips found hers, gently moving against them. "You're my whole world."

"I love you so much. Making love is so much more for me than making a baby. I'm sorry if I made you feel like that was all I wanted from you." She snuggled contentedly in his arms.

Robbie ran his hands over her body. "I got wrapped up in the thought of our baby, and hearing that I won't be able to give that to you wrecked me." He nipped at her neck. "I took that out on you, and I shouldn't have. Forgive me?" Their kisses grew more passionate.

Jenny rubbed the growing bulge in his boxers. "You don't need to ask." She guided his hand between her legs. "Make love to me."

Robbie eased her satin robe over her shoulders and leaned forward to kiss her neck as he ran his hands over her skin, the same as she had done to him. "Come here." He patted the pillow, and Jenny lay beside him. He rolled onto his side to face her. Stroking her back, he felt his desire for her rising. "I've been afraid I wouldn't be able to... perform." He grimaced. "You can tell me I'm being silly."

Jenny moved her hand back to his obvious erection. "This says you're being silly." She smiled as she stroked him.

"There wasn't much going on last week."

"It's going on now. Make love to me," she repeated.

Robbie rolled on top of her and let her guide his cock between her legs. It felt like the first time they'd had sex all those years ago. They were gentle with each other until each of them sensed the other was close, and they gave in to the passion, ending in orgasms that hit first for Jenny and seconds later for Robbie.

She clung to him and whispered into his ear, "We're going to be okay."

Chapter Fifteen

Welcoming Tally

Caden

CADEN WHISTLED AS HE walked home from the hospital. Indian summer was going strong, and he drank in the vivid fall colors of the leaves, which were enhanced by the blue sky. Quinn had been living with him for almost three weeks, and it was everything he'd hoped for. Throughout August and September, they had spent almost every night together, but it had involved a lot of time on the road and a lot of juggling.

Her move-in had been seamless. Even her cat, Max, was coping well with Aurora, the kitten Caden had adopted to ease his loneliness back in the spring. From what he had heard, everyone at the hospital loved Quinn, and she spoke enthusiastically about the work. When their schedules allowed, they walked to and from the hospital together, but she hadn't worked that day, and he couldn't wait to get home to her.

Caden found her relaxing on the terrace off the living room. He leaned down to kiss her lips.

"Do you know how much I love being here, waiting for you at the end of the day?" She gave a wide smile and patted the lounger next to her. "Join me."

"Let me change first."

He was back in five minutes, wearing shorts and a long-sleeved T-shirt and carrying two glasses of wine.

Quinn reached for one of the glasses as he sat down.

"What did the city have for you today?" He loved hearing about her exploration of the area he'd grown up in.

"The morning was so warm that I had a cup of coffee out here, then I worked out."

Caden's brownstone had a gym and sauna on the first floor, and Quinn worked out every day, sometimes by herself and sometimes with Caden. "It's so nice not having to drive to a gym. After my workout, I had breakfast out here, then I visited two bookstores before I met Jen for lunch."

"How was she?"

"Not bad. They have an appointment next week to get the results from the tests they've done and talk about the next steps.

We ate at a Greek café. I love having so many cuisines to pick from. Part of me feels like I'll never need to travel again."

"That's what I tried to tell you on our first date. The city has everything I want. Especially with you here."

"I said 'part of me.'" She grinned. "My wanderlust has not been totally squashed." She moved from her lounger to squeeze in next to him. "But I love it."

He brought his lips to hers, and she opened her mouth, inviting his tongue in. As their kisses intensified, he rubbed her back. "We haven't christened this terrace yet." One hand made its way under her shirt. "You're hot."

"Mm-hmm." She swung her leg over his to straddle him then shoved his shirt up and stroked his chest. "You can make me hotter."

"Challenge accepted." Caden fluttered kisses down her neck until he reached her breasts. His tongue circled her nipple, teasing her until she was squirming in his lap, begging him to do more. Just as his teeth replaced his tongue, his watch buzzed with a phone call. "Damn." He glanced down. "It's Rob. He doesn't usually call."

Quinn nodded for him to answer.

"Hey, Rob. What's up?"

"Brooke's in labor. They dropped Liam off on their way to the hospital."

"Time for Operation Birth a Baby." Caden smiled at Quinn. "It's a little early." Brooke's due date was six days away.

A few weeks earlier, Brooke had expressed her concerns about how Danny would cope while she was in labor. She had labored for twenty-four hours with Liam before he came in a rush at the end. Brooke's mother had been part of her birth team, but this time, her parents were on an extended trip to Spain, where her father was working. On a weekend when Danny was traveling with the Patriots, she'd had a discussion with Caden, Quinn, Rob, and Jennifer.

"I'm going to be totally honest with you," she'd begun. "I need your help when I go into labor." She looked at Rob and Jennifer. "I know this is hard for you."

Jen put her hand on Brooke's. "It is. But we're happy and excited for you." She looked at Robbie, and he nodded. "What can we do?"

"Can you keep Liam?" She started tearing up. "This is difficult with neither Danny's nor my family here. We had so much help when Liam was born."

Robbie put his hand on top of Jenny's. "We love having Liam. It's not a problem. And neither is anything else."

"Thank you." She exhaled. "I don't know how Danny is going to handle labor, especially if it takes as long as it did with Liam. Cade, Quinn and I have already talked about this. It would be a big help if you could be at the hospital. Quinn said she'd hold my hand so Danny could take a break. Could you be in the waiting room with him? That will keep him on an even keel."

Caden wrapped his arms around her. "Of course I can do that. I hate that you have to ask."

"I know. He's so unpredictable. I don't enjoy talking about him behind his back, but I need to know that my ducks are in a row." She'd smiled at them. "You guys are the best."

And suddenly, it was go time. Quinn hopped off Caden's lap as he wrapped up the call with Rob.

"We'll head to the hospital now, and I'll keep you posted."

Caden kissed the top of Quinn's head. "No christening the terrace tonight."

Quinn shook her head. "It's okay. I love being part of a baby being born."

"Me too."

"Hey, hey, Mama. How's it going?" Caden asked as he and Quinn walked into Brooke's room together.

"I've had contractions off and on since this morning. They were getting more regular, and just as Danny got home from work, my water broke. The doctor said to come in, so here we are."

"She was at five centimeters when they checked her." Danny rubbed Brooke's back. "The doc wanted her at the hospital because of how fast things moved after her water broke with Liam."

"And because it's my second. I hope this doesn't take as long as he—whoa, there's one." Brooke grimaced until the contraction subsided.

Danny gave her some ice chips. "You may regret volunteering to hold her hand, Quinn. I think she's broken some of my fingers." He grinned at Brooke.

At the next check, she measured six centimeters, but two hours passed without her contractions progressing. Danny and Caden played cards while Quinn chatted softly with Brooke. "I met Cade and Danny the same day, when I walked into Intro to Art. They both thought it would be an easy A."

Danny spoke up. "I put more effort into that class than all my other ones combined that semester. And still only got a B."

Brooke breathed through a contraction, then said, "I could have had either of them, and I had to choose the ginger. And now here I am, waiting for this redheaded demon to be born."

Danny got up and kissed her lightly. "That hope of quicker labor isn't getting very far." He put his hand on her belly and kept it there when another contraction hit.

"That's three in a row at four minutes apart." Quinn was timing them. "I think you're making progress."

Brooke nodded. "Danny, why don't you and Cade take a break. Then you'll be ready for the big show."

Caden watched the relief wash over Danny's face.

"Thanks, babe. We won't be far." Danny stood at the door, waiting for Caden, who stopped to kiss Quinn and squeeze Brooke's hand.

Danny paced around the waiting room. "It's hard to watch her in pain."

Caden nodded.

"You don't need to tell me she doesn't get a break," Danny said defensively.

"I get it. When it's Quinn's and my turn, I'm going to have a hard time seeing her suffer. Let's get some coffee."

"I'd rather have this." Danny took a flask out of his jacket pocket.

"What the fuck are you doing?" Caden was shocked to see Danny unscrewing the top and tipping the flask into his mouth.

"Taking the edge off." Danny wiped his mouth and put the flask back in his pocket. "Don't get all judgy on me."

"Judgy?" Caden was relieved they were the only ones in the waiting room. "Your wife is in there, going through hell to give you the greatest gift in the world, and you need to take the fucking *edge* off?"

"Yeah, I do." Danny looked at him defiantly.

"What the hell has happened to you?" Caden shook his head. "Where's the person who's been my best friend since we learned to walk?"

Danny continued to pace. Finally, he turned to face Caden. "Not everyone has the golden lives you and Rob do."

135

"Are you fucking kidding me? My life was real golden when I walked in on Mary fucking some rando in our bed. And when I discovered she'd been cheating on me for most of our years together. Or the most golden moment of all, when I started having panic attacks and wandered out into the snow barefoot." Caden was struggling to contain his anger. "Maybe you should ask Rob how golden his life is."

Danny scoffed. "What? Because Jen isn't pregnant yet? That's a tragedy?" He took another swallow from the flask then sat down and closed his eyes.

Caden took several deep breaths, trying to bury the fury he was feeling.

They sat in silence for over an hour until Quinn walked in. Caden knew she could feel the tension in the room, and he read the question in her eyes. He raised his hands, partly in surrender and partly to let her know he'd fill her in later.

"Danny," Quinn said urgently.

He opened his eyes and scrambled up from the chair he'd been slouched in. "Yeah?"

"Things moved faster after you left. She's almost at ten and will start pushing soon. She wants you."

He walked into the hallway then turned back to Quinn. "Are you coming with me?"

"No. This is a moment for you and Brooke. We'll wait here." She pulled a chair close to Caden and took one of his hands as she sat down. "What's going on?"

Caden squeezed her hand. "Let's move over to that couch. I need to feel you next to me."

They stood, and he wrapped his arms around her. She was a comfort. He rested his chin on her head then finally broke his hold on her and moved to the couch. He put his arm over her shoulders, holding her close. "You can't imagine how much I need this. Danny has a flask in his pocket, and when I asked if he wanted coffee, he whipped it out and took a hit from it."

Quinn's eyes widened.

"Because he needed to take the edge off." Caden scoffed. "I'm furious, and I don't even know who he is anymore."

"He hasn't always drunk like this?"

"No. God, no."

"Tell me more about Danny. And about Brooke. Could she have had you?" Quinn squeezed his hand.

"Danny's parents lived next door to mine, so I've known him all my life. He's the youngest of three. His parents were a lot more permissive than mine, so he was more of a rule breaker than I ever thought of being." Caden ran a hand through his hair. "He was more of everything than I was. More sarcastic, more of a joker, more of a risk-taker, and significantly more of a hothead. It was like he had to have the fiery temper to go with the red hair. But he never stayed angry for long, and he was loyal to a fault. Danny always had my back. He was the brother I didn't have. We all drank too much in college and, like everything else, Danny pushed the boundary on that too."

Caden looked at his watch. "Do you think we've got a bit of time?" When Quinn nodded, he said, "Let's get that coffee."

When they sat back down, he continued, "We were both attracted to Brooke." Remembering that time in his life felt good. "Hell, we were eighteen and attracted to every girl we saw." He grinned at Quinn. "I never told you I was an angel."

She giggled. "Nope. I think you told me the opposite."

"That sounds right. Brooke had something extra about her. I think part of it was that she took the course seriously, as opposed to us and almost everyone else. Danny fell a lot harder than I did, so I never considered asking her out. She became a good friend, almost another sister. Her relationship with Danny was volatile, and I was her sounding board when they fought."

"Did they ever break up?"

"No. They got married when we were twenty-four, after they finished grad school. He's not the Danny I've known my entire life. It started when he didn't get the promotion he expected with the Patriots. I feel bad because I wasn't around. I withdrew from everything after I left you. Maybe if I'd been there, he wouldn't have gotten this bad."

"You had your own stuff you were dealing with."

"I did." He kissed her. "I'm at a loss. He made a crack about how Rob and I lead golden lives. I've never seen him with a complete lack of empathy." He was silent for several minutes. "I can't believe he's drinking when Brooke's on the verge of giving birth. Things can't continue like this."

A nurse came into the room. "Your friends would like to see you." She was smiling.

Danny was lying on the bed next to Brooke, who was cradling a baby wearing a pink cap.

"A girl?" Caden asked.

He and Quinn crowded the bed.

Danny answered, "Meet Tallulah Maeve. We're going to call her Tally."

"That's beautiful," Quinn said with a sigh.

"Do you want to hold her?" Wonder filled Brooke's voice.

"Are you sure?"

"She's already nursed. I think she'd like to meet her uncle Caden and aunt Quinn. Which one of you wants her first?"

"Let Quinn." Caden studied Danny, who showed none of the agitation he had in the waiting room. The sight of Quinn holding the newborn stirred desires he hadn't dared to acknowledge. He edged closer to Quinn. "Is she a red-haired demon?"

Danny replied, "Her hair is darker than Liam's was. She's probably going to be more auburn. A nice combination of Brooke and me." He leaned down to kiss his wife.

"She's so special," Quinn murmured, with tears in her eyes. "This is the first time I've been referred to as an aunt." She looked at Caden. "I know you want to hold her."

He took her and expertly cuddled her to his chest. "Hey, Tally. We're excited you're here."

"Did everything go okay?" Quinn asked.

"Yes," Brooke answered. "Much quicker than with Liam. I could do this again." She leaned against Danny.

"We always talked about three." Danny put his arm around Brooke's shoulders then looked at Caden. "I texted Rob to let him know. They'll bring Liam in the morning."

"We should leave so you can sleep." Caden lowered Tally into Danny's arms. "Keep us posted about when you go home. Liam's going to be so excited." He took Quinn's hand. "We love you guys."

While Caden and Quinn waited for the elevator, he said, "That's the Danny I know. Maybe he was just stressed about the birth."

"I hope so. He was more like the man you introduced me to on New Year's Eve." Her eyes twinkled. "Seeing you holding Tallulah started my lady parts buzzing."

"Let's go home and finish what we started."

Chapter Sixteen

A Path Forward

Jenny

"I CAN'T WAIT TO see my sister." Liam was walking between Jenny and Robbie, holding their hands. "Can you swing me?"

Robbie grinned at Jenny, and together, they lifted the little boy off the floor.

"Higher, Uncle Rob." Liam giggled as he swung between them.

Jenny glanced at Robbie, and he smiled at her, but the smile didn't reach his eyes. She remembered their conversation on the Fourth of July and knew today would be hard for him.

Liam ran into Brooke's room. "Mommy!"

Danny scooped him up. "Shhhh, buddy. Your baby sister is asleep. Can you soften your voice?"

"I want to see her. Are you taking a nap, Mommy?" He squirmed to get out of Danny's arms. Once on the floor, he peeked into the Isolette. "She's little." He moved to the side of the bed and reached his hands to Brooke, letting her know he wanted to lie next to her.

Rob looked at Brooke, silently asking if she was okay with the toddler joining her.

She nodded with a smile, and Rob lifted him onto the bed.

Liam snuggled next to her. "Uncle Rob helped me make a Lego dinosaur last night."

"I bet that was fun." As Brooke spoke, soft mewing sounds started in the Isolette.

Jen asked, "Is it okay if I pick her up?"

"Of course," Brooke answered quickly.

She lifted the baby and cradled her close to her chest, losing herself for a moment, overtaken by the fresh baby scent and the warmth emanating from the baby's tiny body. Tally opened her eyes and looked directly at Jen, whose heart thumped with affection for her. She stroked Tally's cheek. "You are so beautiful," she murmured. For a moment, Jen was unaware of anyone else in the room. It was just her and the newborn.

Tally mewed again, and Brooke said, "She's probably ready to nurse again. You guys can stay." She extended her arms to take the baby.

Liam's eyes widened as Brooke brought Tally to her breast, and she patiently answered all of his questions while Jen and Rob moved to the other side of the room to chat with Danny.

I want to experience that so much. Jenny's heart ached at the thought of what she might never have. *Robbie and I have never talked about breastfeeding. We've only discussed how much we want a baby and what a hard time we're having. I can't ever let him know how strongly I'd like to nourish our baby that way.*

After Tally finished nursing and her diaper had been changed, Danny held her out to Rob. "Everyone has held her but you. Time to step up."

Rob's large hands enveloped her, and he held her comfortably.

"I forgot what a natural you are." Brooke watched him.

Rocking gently, he replied, "You never met all my younger siblings. There were plenty of them, and I was pressed into service. It's one of those skills you never forget."

Liam stayed with his parents when Robbie and Jenny left, making their way silently out of the hospital.

Finally, Robbie said, "She's beautiful. Lucky girl, she looks like Brooke."

Jenny took his hand. "That was hard, huh?"

"Yup."

They walked several blocks with no further words.

"I tell my clients and guardian ad litem kids all the time that life's not fair, yet that was all I could think in that hospital room.

It's not fair that Danny and Brooke have two, and we don't have any." He dropped Jenny's hand and put his arm around her shoulders. "I sound like a petulant child. You don't have to tell me."

"No, I've had the same feelings." She moved closer to him. As they passed a children's clothing store, she slowed. "We need to get a gift for Tally. We agreed to shop after the baby was born."

Robbie stopped, but before they entered the store, he said, "Cade called me this morning. You were in the shower."

"Did he want to talk about Danny's behavior in the waiting room?"

"You talked to Quinn." He turned to look at her.

Jenny nodded. "She said he was livid."

"He was still angry when he talked to me, even though Danny was fine when he and Quinn saw them after Tally was born."

"What can you do?"

Robbie shrugged. "Cade said he's going to be watching, and he'll confront Danny if he thinks the drinking continues to escalate. We've all been ignoring it. Even Brooke. Cade thinks it's time to take action."

"Whoa. Maybe the baby being born will snap him out of it. He seemed like the old Danny just now."

"Maybe." Robbie cocked his head toward the shop door. "Let's go see what we can find for Miss Tallulah."

Late the next day, Robbie followed Jenny into Dr. Kerr's office. It had been three weeks since he went to the first appointment. He and Jenny had undergone complete physicals and had blood drawn. He'd provided a sperm sample, and a week ago, he'd had a scrotal ultrasound. Today, they would get the results of all the testing and find out if there was any hope of conceiving a child. They were both anxious, and it had been a long twenty-four hours since they had taken Liam to the hospital to meet his baby sister.

Jed escorted them to a comfortable room that looked like a high-end hotel lobby. Jenny felt like she had walked into a sunset, as the room was decorated in warm shades of amber, pink, and orange. A couch and two comfortable armchairs sat in the front part, and a large wooden desk was in the back.

Ivy was waiting for them and stood to shake their hands. "Welcome. We use this office when we meet to discuss the results. It isn't necessary to take vitals, and we try to make everyone comfortable." She extended her hand toward the couch. "Please have a seat."

Jenny flashed back to her first appointment with Ivy. She hadn't anticipated the level of testing. *I can't believe how naive I was when I thought we would walk into an office and have IUI done right away.* Besides a physical and blood work, she'd had another transvaginal ultrasound and tests to look at her uterus and fallopian tubes. If she hadn't thought so before, she now knew they were officially on an infertility journey. The

HSG—for the first time in her life, Jenny was thankful for the alphabet soup of abbreviations—had been uncomfortable, and she'd spent the evening afterward on the couch with a heating pad.

It shattered Robbie to watch her suffering, and she was heartbroken at his distress. *What a mess we've been since we found out he's sterile. Having Liam was a good break for us. But at least we're facing it together.*

They sat down, and Jenny reached for his hand.

Jed spoke first. "I wish we could tell you that your original semen analysis was wrong, but we can't. Our results are basically the same. Your sperm count is low and unlikely to result in a pregnancy from intercourse alone, but we don't believe the motility is an issue."

Robbie's grip on Jenny's hand tightened.

"Your results were good, Jen," Ivy added. "We saw the fibroids Dr. Randolph mentioned in her notes, but we don't think they're of any consequence."

They paused, obviously giving Jenny and Rob a moment to absorb the news.

Thank goodness she didn't say there's no reason I can't conceive and have a normal pregnancy. That would have devastated Robbie. He was staring straight ahead, still holding her hand. She squeezed his hand, and he turned to her with a sad smile.

Jenny asked, "What's next?"

"Your best chance for conception is with IVF, but you mentioned wanting to try IUI, and we certainly can do that. It's less invasive, and we can do it the next time you're ovulating."

"My period started three days ago, so in a little less than two weeks?" Jenny felt a glimmer of hope.

"Yes," Jed answered. "I want to caution you to keep your expectations realistic. The probability of success is not high, and we will only try twice. If you haven't conceived by New Year's, then it will be time to explore IVF."

His voice was soft and comforting, and Jen understood why he was the one talking. His wife was much more matter-of-fact.

Robbie spoke for the first time since they had entered the office. "What do we need to do to get ready for that?"

Ivy smiled. "Go home and have lots of sex."

"Beg pardon?" Robbie looked at Jenny with wide eyes.

"I know your instinct is going to be not to ejaculate to 'save up' your sperm, but we want fresh, young sperm to use in the procedure. So you need to go ahead and enjoy each other. Everything else you need to know is in the packet of information we'll give you to take home."

Jed followed up on what Ivy had said. "For more than a year, you've focused on trying to make a baby. This is your opportunity to get back to enjoying each other. That's important to your relationship. And a strong relationship is going to be important as you go forward."

Jenny smiled at Robbie as they stood.

When they were outside, Robbie took the folder Jenny had been handed as they left the office. "That was not what I expected."

His voice had the hint of fun that Jenny had been missing. "Me either. How do you feel?"

"I'm excited that we have the IUI on our radar, pleased that the *only* problem is the low sperm count and not the motility, and kinda liking the prescription for lots of sex."

"Me too."

"Can you forgive me for the crack I made about our doing a science experiment? I've never been more excited about science, and you know very well that was never my favorite subject."

"I know you said that when your emotions were running rampant. We should make a pact that anything said in the heat of the moment gets a pass. When we get home, let's go through all this information then get going on that prescription."

Chapter Seventeen

A Night To Celebrate

Caden

CADEN RODE THE ELEVATOR to the ground floor of the hotel with his heart pounding and remembered it racing the same way the night he'd ended things with Quinn. He smiled. Tonight was going to have a very different outcome. At least, he hoped so. Hank and Mel Michaels, Quinn's parents, had settled in their hotel room, and the other guests would arrive soon.

He was walking by the lobby bar, heading for the exit, when a head of blond hair caught his attention.

The blonde shrieked, "Dr. Caden Brady! You'd better stop." Liz, the dynamo who had been Quinn's roommate in Honduras, threw herself into his arms.

As Caden hugged her, he looked over her head to where her boyfriend, Marc, stood.

When Liz let go, Caden extended his hand to Marc. "Good to see you again."

Marc had also been a nurse at the clinic. "It is. Even if we *are* in Boston." Marc lived in New Jersey, and the two men had engaged in a running argument over whether New York City or Boston had the better sports teams. "Do you have time to have a drink with us?"

"Yes, Quinn won't be home until close to four."

The bartender was a friend of Caden's, and he asked, "Jameson?"

Caden nodded. "Three, please." He looked at Marc and Liz to make sure they were okay with his choice.

"Nice upgrade from what we drank at the clinic." Marc knocked his back. "I hear I should have stayed another week so I could have flown home first class." He raised a finger to order another shot.

Liz put her hand on his arm. "Stop. We flew up here first class, and our room is gorgeous. Thank you, Caden."

"I'm learning to enjoy the money I have by indulging other people."

Marc raised his glass. "You want another?"

Caden shook his head.

"I was just giving you a hard time." Marc put his arm around Liz's waist. "We appreciate it all. You know we would have come anyway."

"Glad to hear that. It should be a fun weekend."

"Does Quinn have any idea?" Liz asked.

"I don't think so."

"Are you sure she's going to say yes?"

And Marc followed up with, "What'll you do if she doesn't?"

"Be very embarrassed." Caden chuckled. "We've talked about it. I think we're on the same page." He ran a hand through his hair. "I need to head out. I'll see you later. O'Malley's Pub. It's easy to find."

Once he'd reached home, he turned on the fireplace in the den and sank onto the love seat. Marc had given voice to the anxiety Caden felt. He and Quinn had discussed marriage and spending the rest of their lives together, but no specific details. After he popped the question, they would go to the large party he had planned, and he hoped he wouldn't be embarrassed and disappointed.

His mind drifted back to his proposal to Mary. She had orchestrated the entire thing and made all her expectations clear. Caden had foolishly allowed himself to be manipulated. That was a major part of why he wanted to surprise Quinn.

He stretched out and replaced his memories of Mary with ones of his moments with Quinn—seeing her for the first time at the lobby bar; the day they'd spent together at the conference, breaking the ice; the first weekend they'd spent together; making love for the first time and all the times after; riding the chairlift to the top of Burke Mountain to declare his love for her; the shock of seeing her in Honduras; the moment when they finally reunited; and now, the walks they took through the city every night and lying on the couch with her in his arms while they watched his kitten harass Max. He loved her completely and couldn't imagine a future without her.

"Wake up, sleepyhead." Quinn kissed his lips.

His eyes popped open. "Not really asleep. Just thinking." He pulled her down on top of him.

"Stop. Who knows how many germs these scrubs have on them? I want to take a quick shower, then we can go for our walk before dinner."

Later, Caden put on a fleece vest over his Henley and watched Quinn pull on leggings and a heavy sweater. When they left the brownstone, he turned toward the bridge that would take them across the Charles River and into Cambridge. "Where are we going?"

"It's a pleasant night. We've never gone to Cambridge after dark, and neither of us has to work again until Monday, so I thought a longer walk would be fun."

"Okay. Are you going to O'Malley's? It's Friday night."

He appreciated the way she insisted he maintain his friendships. "Maybe later. I'll reach out to the guys. Can you believe

Tally is two weeks old? Danny's been better when we visited, and I don't know if he's ready to leave Brooke. Rob and Jen are going to do the IUI in the next few days, so he may be abstaining from alcohol." He grinned at her. "You could be stuck with me tonight." *I'm lying through my teeth.*

"What a horrible fate." She kissed him. "Rob still hasn't told Danny that he's sterile. Jen's having a hard time not telling Brooke where things stand."

Caden shook his head. "I'm hoping he'll be comfortable enough to tell him soon."

They walked along, chatting about everything and nothing.

"Did I ever tell you that Sam and I Ubered over to Harvard the night before that conference started?" Quinn asked. "We were both nervous about not knowing where we were going and wanted to get our bearings."

"No, you hadn't told me that. Did it help?"

"A little. But what really eased my anxiety was this very handsome doctor who bought me a chai after some rude kid knocked mine out of my hand."

He put his arm around her shoulders and pulled her close. "I'm glad someone did something so kind for you."

When they reached the Harvard campus, Quinn started trying to identify the building where they had met. As she looked around, Caden slowed down a bit, so she was ahead of him. "Is this the infamous building where you saw me getting out of the

Uber?" She turned to ask again, "Cade, is this where... Oh my God!"

He was on one knee, looking up at her. "Quinn Michaels, a year ago, you walked out of an Uber and into my heart. I love you, and I want you to always be a part of my life. I want to take care of you and have you take care of me. I want you to have my children. I want all of it with you. Will you marry me?"

Quinn put her hand over her mouth and tried to blink back the tears that had started when she realized what he was doing. "Yes, yes, yes! I love you so much, and I want all of that with you too!"

Caden stood, took her hand, and slipped the ring he'd been carrying onto her finger. She threw her arms around him, and he hugged her tightly.

As she caught her breath, a limousine pulled up. "For us?" she asked.

"For us. We've got a party to get to."

The limo driver opened the door for them and, once they were inside, popped open a champagne bottle then poured and handed them flutes.

Caden tapped his glass against hers. "To us." After they'd both taken a swallow, he said, "I'm glad you said yes."

The love Quinn felt for him radiated from her eyes. "How else would I have answered? I want everything you said—forever and kids. Of course I'd say yes."

"Wasn't sure how you'd feel about being surprised."

"It was perfect."

When they walked into O'Malley's, instead of the usual Friday night crowd, the familiar faces of people important to them were waiting. All of Caden's family, Quinn's parents, Robbie and Jen, Danny and Brooke, doctors Caden was close to, and some of his hockey teammates. She saw Ashley and her fiancé, Aaron, from Hanover, standing near the bar.

"Oh my God." Quinn had her hand over her mouth. She looked up at Caden. "You planned all this?"

He nodded.

"I'm dumbstruck." Her parents were the closest to her, and she hugged them. "I'm engaged!"

Friends crowded around, wanting to see her ring and clapping Caden on the shoulder to congratulate him.

When Ashley and Aaron approached, Izzy and Ethan were right behind. "Izzy, I didn't even see you at first." She looked at the women, who were two of her closest friends. "Thank you for making the trip down here. It means so much."

Izzy answered, "Caden made it very hard to say no."

Quinn cocked her head.

Ashley explained, "We have a room at the hotel you stayed at last fall. I think most of the out-of-town people do."

"What did you do?" She grinned at him.

Caden winked. "We're staying in the penthouse for the weekend, and I figured you'd like to spend some time with your people."

Caden's parents were next to hug them, then his sisters. After they all had a turn, Liz and Marc stepped out of the shadows.

"Liz!" Quinn reached out to hug her. "I've missed you."

"Same, girl. Same. Whoever would have thought you'd end up engaged to the very hot but standoffish Dr. Brady?"

"I'm going to put that standoffish rumor to rest this weekend." Caden grinned at her.

After greeting everyone, they spent the rest of the evening eating, drinking, playing darts, and visiting. Caden delighted in watching Quinn sneak peeks at the ring on her finger.

As the party wound down, Danny and Brooke came over to say goodbye. Brooke hugged first Quinn then Caden. "My mother arrived just in time to take care of Tally. I'm so happy for you two and glad we could be here."

Danny hugged Quinn and fist-bumped his lifelong best friend. "Happy for you, buddy. And by the way, I'm never playing darts with Cathleen again."

Caden looked at his younger sister, and she raised her hand in an innocent wave. "She mopped the floor with me back in January."

He had arranged transportation back to the hotel for all the out-of-town people, and when they left, only Robbie and Jen remained.

Rob embraced Quinn. "We're happy for you, darlin'. Caden's the best, but you already know that." He let her go and turned to Cade, wrapping him in an embrace. "I'm glad everything worked out."

"Me too."

Jenny hugged them both, echoed Robbie's well-wishes, then added, "I think the IUI will be tomorrow. Hold some good thoughts for us."

Caden and Quinn made their way to the top floor of the hotel, and when he opened the door to the penthouse, she jumped into his arms. "You are amazing. That was so much fun."

He held her, relishing the feel of her against his body. Finally, he let her go. "Now we can have our own private celebration." He threw his vest onto a chair and tugged on Quinn's sweater. "I want to make love to my fiancée."

"I like that idea." She stood on tiptoe to reach his lips.

They moved together, and Caden opened his mouth, wanting more.

His hands started on her back and drifted to her butt. When he stroked it, Quinn moaned. They separated, and Caden shoved her leggings to the floor then lifted her sweater over her head. "I watched you in those leggings all night, and as gorgeous as you are in them, I couldn't wait for this moment."

He pulled his Henley off, and Quinn unzipped his jeans.

Her hand found his erection, and she pushed him onto the bed. After she'd pulled off his jeans, she knelt in front of him and took his cock in her mouth. While she sucked, she fondled his balls, and Caden struggled to remain still.

"Babe, you know I love what you're doing, but that's not how I want it tonight. Come up here."

Quinn crawled on top of him and landed with his cock against her clit. She squirmed against it. "Is this how you want it?"

"Close," he spat out. He ran his hands up and down her back before moving them to her breasts. When he thumbed her nipple, it hardened in response.

"Close to where you want to be, or close to an orgasm?" Quinn whispered.

"Both." He moved his hands from her breasts to her hips and lifted her up. "I want to be inside." Lowering her onto his cock, he resisted the urge to thrust against her. "This is the best. I love you so much." His hands stayed on her hips, and when her squirming increased, he slid one between them so he could stroke her clit.

She sighed and shifted on his erection. "You know what that does. I'm so close. Come with me."

That was all Caden needed. They moved together, exploding in thunderous orgasms. Quinn collapsed onto him, and he rolled them onto their sides, leaving his cock buried inside.

When he caught his breath, he said, "We're going to have an amazing life together."

"Mmmm." Quinn snuggled closer to him. "When do you want to get married?"

"Tomorrow."

"Seriously?"

Caden moved away so he could see her face. "Maybe a little serious. I don't want to wait a long time. What about you?"

"I don't either, and you already know I don't want a big wedding." She reached up to stroke his cheek. "But I want to enjoy being engaged for a little while. I want to have a few months of referring to you as my fiancé before I start calling you my husband." She grinned. "You're going to be my husband. I'm so happy."

Caden smiled. "Come here, future wife."

They held each other long into the night.

Chapter Eighteen

The First Attempt

Robbie

JENNY SQUEEZED ROBBIE'S HAND as they sat in the waiting room. Because it was Saturday, he had expected they would be the only ones in the office, but there were two other couples. He studied them, wondering what their fertility issues were. His perspective on life had undergone a serious makeover since he and Jenny had started trying to have a baby more than a year ago. He'd always considered himself an empathetic person, but their journey had made him realize he knew nothing about what people were going through. Finding out he was sterile had hammered that home even more. He'd never again assume he knew anything about anyone's life.

"Last night was fun. I liked Quinn's friends."

Robbie knew Jenny was trying to break the tension in the room. "I did too. It's good to see Cade happy. And it was nice to have a distraction."

A medical assistant led them to an exam room. She had barely finished recording their vital statistics when Dr. Kerr walked in. "Good morning." She flashed a bright smile. "From your temperature and the chart you've been keeping, I think today's our day. You can undress, and I'll check your cervix, then we'll do the transvaginal ultrasound. If everything looks good, it'll be your turn, Rob. You'll give us your sample, we'll wash it, then it will be go time for the procedure. I know we've gone over all of this before, but I like to be sure we're all on the same page. Do you have questions?"

Jenny turned from the doctor to Robbie, and he shook his head. "I think we're good," she said.

"We do everything right in this room, so you don't have to traipse around the building. If you're comfortable, you can stay together or go back to the waiting room if we're not doing something that requires your presence."

"We're in this together," Robbie answered.

"I thought that was what you'd say." Ivy flashed another smile. "Jen, you can change, and I'll be back in a few minutes."

Jenny put on a peach-colored gown made of jersey then climbed onto the exam table, and Robbie sat in a chair next to her.

She took his hand. "This gown is not typical."

"Neither is this room, from my limited exposure to doctors." The room was a darker shade of peach than the gown, and the furniture was warm maple. It had all the usual devices a doctor's office required, but also had family-centric artwork on the walls along with motivational posters.

"I'm glad we ended up here." Jenny adjusted her position. "Wait until you see me with my feet in the stirrups. Most undignified position in the world."

"We're both going to be in some undignified positions." He leaned over to kiss her. "We're going to focus on the prize."

Dr. Kerr had Jen get into position while she wrapped the speculum in a warm towel. She spoke softly, describing each step. "Are you doing okay?"

"Yup. You warming that speculum is one of the nicest things ever."

"Jed and I went through it all, and we swore we would alleviate as much discomfort as possible when we opened our practice. Some things are unavoidable, like this little pinch." She paused. "Sorry. But we know how difficult this is, and our aim is to make our patients relaxed and comfy." She moved back. "Your cervix looks good. You can stay there. The ultrasound tech will be right in."

After she'd left, Robbie blew out a long breath. "One step down." He massaged Jenny's shoulders. "Did that hurt, what she just did?"

"Not really. This next thing will."

"You didn't look undignified at all. You're the most beautiful woman in the world."

He had her wrapped in his arms when the technician walked in.

"Sorry."

Robbie jumped away, embarrassed. He sat down and flashed Jenny a grin. The exam started, and he could tell by Jenny's expression when the tech hit a sensitive spot. Their hands were joined, and she gripped tightly while the tech was working. *I hate that she has to go through this. Nothing about my contribution has been painful in any way.*

The tech finished and left the room.

"Whooo." Jenny exhaled. "I'm glad that's done. It's nice having you here."

After a while, Ivy came back in. "Everything looks great. I'd say you're going to ovulate within the next twenty-four hours. And that's perfect. It's your turn now, Rob. Everything you need is on the table. I'm going to dim the lights and leave. One of you can let me know when the sample is ready." She winked as she tapped the light switch. "It's a good day to make a baby."

Jenny climbed off the table and into his lap. "That's from *Grey's Anatomy*. One of the surgeons used to say, 'It's a good day to save lives,' before he started an operation. I really like Dr. Kerr."

"Me too." They kissed for a few minutes. "We need to get this show started."

He left for the bathroom then came back in a pair of black pajama pants.

"Do you want help?" she asked.

"What you did the first time would be nice."

She smiled as she pushed the pants to the floor and grasped his cock. It hardened at her touch, and she stroked him until he replaced her hand with his.

A few minutes later, he came with a groan and leaned back in the chair. "Swim hard, guys," he whispered.

A technician retrieved the sample, and Ivy returned forty-five minutes later. "Okay, we're all set for the big finale. There will be some pain when the catheter goes through your cervix into the uterus. You keep holding her hand, Rob. This won't take more than ten minutes."

She was true to her word. Ten minutes later, she was withdrawing the speculum. "I'm going to give you some time. Don't rush to get dressed. Relax for a bit," she said before leaving.

"Did it hurt?" Robbie asked as he stood beside her.

"It's a little crampy."

"Can you roll onto your side? I'll rub your back." He frequently did that when she had cramps during her period. He was still rubbing circles on her lower back when Dr. Kerr returned.

"That cramping shouldn't last long. Try a heating pad when you get home. Then have sex."

Rob was skeptical. "Are you sure that's a good idea?"

"I am. Intercourse today, tomorrow, and even the day after will cover the period when Jen is ovulating. That will put more sperm into play. And psychologically, it will be good for you."

"It won't gum up the procedure?"

"No, trust me. Take a pregnancy test two weeks from today. Schedule an appointment before you leave. If your test is positive, we'll follow up with a blood test, and if it's not, we'll discuss the next steps. You know we're all rooting for you."

"I'm going to lie down until this subsides." Jenny stripped off her clothes and crawled under the covers.

Robbie found their heating pad, plugged it in, and placed it on her abdomen.

"That feels good." She sounded sleepy.

"Are you tired?" Robbie asked as he undressed.

"Kind of wiped out emotionally. How about you?"

"The same." He joined her under the blanket.

"You don't have to lie here. You probably have other things you want to do."

Robbie settled her against him. "There's *nothing* else I'd rather do." He listened to her breathing. *I want this to work more than I've ever wanted anything in my whole life.*

"Robbie." Jenny's whisper pulled him up from the depths of sleep.

He shook his head, trying to awaken. "I didn't mean to fall asleep. Are you feeling better?"

She rolled onto her side, bringing her body against his, and moved her hand between his legs. "Yes." Her fingers wrapped around his cock. "We've got homework to do."

Robbie rubbed her back as his erection grew. His hands lingered on her favorite spots, and she squirmed in response. He reached for her clit and played with it, easing his fingers closer to entering her. Normally, he wouldn't hesitate. He'd have two fingers inside, hitting all the sensitive areas, making her moan with pleasure as she thrust against him. But today felt different. "I'm nervous." *Jesus. Nervous is what fifteen-year-old Robbie was when he made it to home plate with Vickie from geometry. I've never been nervous with Jenny.* "I'm afraid of messing things up. Aren't you?"

"Not at all." Her voice was soft and exuded love. "I want to make love to the most amazing man I've ever met. The one who's always there to hold my hand and tells me I'm beautiful while I'm lying with my feet in stirrups and my legs spread." While she talked, Jenny ran her hands all over his body. She paused at his nipples, and they hardened under her touch.

Stretching to reach, she ran her tongue over the nub, and Robbie shuddered in response.

He waited to see where she would move next. Her touch and her words were soothing, and he felt the anxiety fading while his arousal grew under her leisurely caress. Finally, she let her hand return to his cock, but she didn't rush there either.

Robbie felt like he was on fire. Jenny had banished his nerves, and the only thing he wanted to do was enjoy her body. He put his hand back between her legs, and didn't hesitate. He brushed her clit then slid his fingers inside. She moaned and shifted her hips against him.

Gently, he pushed her down and straddled her. "Hi." He smiled before he ducked his head to play with her nipples.

Her hips shifted again. "I want you inside," she murmured.

"Yes, ma'am." He slid his cock in, thrust a couple of times, then stilled. Being with Jenny was warm, comfortable, and familiar. It was home. "You're my whole heart." He thrust into her and held back until he felt her come then let his orgasm take over.

Afterward, they remained wrapped in each other's arms.

"Thank you," he said.

"I love you. We'll always have us, no matter what."

Chapter Nineteen

Honesty & Heartbreak

Robbie

"I'm excited about seeing Tally. She's almost a month old. But I know it's hard for you." Jenny squeezed Robbie's hand as they walked from the T stop to Danny and Brooke's house. It had been ten days since the procedure.

"I've come to terms with the fact that our friends are going to have babies. It won't be long for Cade and Quinn. We can't isolate ourselves from them."

168

They were almost at the house when Robbie spoke again. "If they ask how things are going, I'm going to tell them."

"Are you sure?"

"Yeah, I should have done it weeks ago. That might have been easier. And I know you want to talk to Brooke." He kissed the top of her head. "So total honesty tonight."

"Okay. But let's avoid the Patriots if we can. That'll just stir Danny up." The football team was not having a good season.

They were chuckling when Danny opened the door. "What's so funny?" Danny asked as Liam attached himself to Rob's leg.

"Hey, little guy." Rob scooped up Liam, deflecting Danny's question. "How's that baby sister of yours?"

"She cries a lot."

"I hear babies do that."

After dinner, Danny went to the fridge. "Beer?" He'd had two with dinner while Rob had stuck to water.

"Nah, I'm good."

Conversation had been easy as they ate. They'd steered clear of football, as the baby and the engagement party absorbed them. But they were about to sit in the living room, and Rob didn't know where the conversation would go. Danny rarely got obnoxious until he'd had four or more drinks, so Rob hoped the beer in his hand was his last. *I'm sterile.* Rob was rehearsing what he'd say if the conversation swung around to their baby journey. *I'd go home now, but I know Jenny wants to spend some time snuggling Tally.*

Danny drained his beer, and Rob watched Brooke frown at him. *She doesn't want him to have another. I wonder how much he's drinking.* He'd been on paternity leave for two weeks and hadn't joined him and Cade at O'Malley's since Tally's birth.

"I was so busy finishing my decorating jobs before Tally's due date I feel like I lost track of everything. You had a doctor's appointment, right? Or maybe more than one."

Jenny was holding the baby, and she looked at Robbie.

Robbie answered Brooke's question. "So, it turns out my swimmers are the problem. My sperm count is low." He could not get out the word *sterile.* He would be the lovable goofball Brooke and Danny knew in college. There was no way he would let them know how devastated he was by the diagnosis.

"I'm so sorry." Brooke's face reflected her distress for them, but he was sure she also wondered why Jenny hadn't already told her. "There must be something you can do."

"There is." Jenny played with Tally's fingers. "We're seeing fertility specialists. A cool husband-and-wife team. There are a bunch of different procedures to try."

"That's rough, man," Danny said. "Hope it works out."

"Yeah. We'll figure it out." Robbie was glad Jenny hadn't gone into the nuts and bolts of what they were doing. He still expected some kind of totally classless response from Danny.

On Thursday morning, Jenny came out of the bathroom and sat on the edge of the bed. She burrowed her hand under the covers to find Robbie's hand. "My period has started."

Robbie's stomach twisted. *Don't let her know how much this upsets you.* He scrambled to a sitting position and hugged her. "I'm sorry, babe."

She buried her face in his shoulders. "We knew it was a long shot."

"Do you want to try again?"

"Let's talk tonight. I need to get ready for work."

"You're going to work?"

"Robbie, I've been going to work when I was on my period since..." She raised her hands in exasperation. "Forever. There's no reason for today to be any different."

"I know." He shrugged. "I don't know what I was thinking."

A crisis at work kept Jen there late, and she wasn't in the mood to talk when she got home. On Friday, she had dinner plans with Brooke and Quinn, and she urged him to meet his friends at O'Malley's.

She needs to talk to her girlfriends. This sucks.

Rob was the first at the pub and had two beers down by the time Caden walked in. "The IUI didn't work. We told Brooke and Danny what's going on, but not the details, and I'm not talking about it with him tonight." He was relieved to get that out and to confide in Caden. He ordered a third beer.

Before Caden could respond, Danny arrived and caught up with Rob in alcohol consumption. And all he did was complain. "I don't know why I took those two weeks off. I came back to a desk covered with crap and probably a thousand emails. You can't imagine how hard it is to put a positive spin on the team this year. The baby's got colic. I was unaware a kid could cry this much. We're both exhausted, and Liam wants more attention than ever. Why the hell did we think another kid was a good idea?"

Rob's blood boiled. *Jenny and I are struggling so hard to have a child, and there's Danny questioning why he and Brooke had another one.* He ordered another beer and turned away from his friends to watch the television over the bar. Danny continued complaining to Caden, and Cade unsuccessfully tried to jolly him into a better mood. Rage built within Rob, and even another beer didn't tamp it down.

I should leave. Is Jenny still crying on the shoulders of her friends? He sent her a text, asking if she was home, and his phone buzzed immediately with a message saying it would be half an hour.

The bartender replaced his empty with a fresh bottle, and Rob took a swallow. *I shouldn't be drinking. We're going to do IUI again, and alcohol isn't good for sperm. Jesus, never did I think that I'd have to give up so many things I enjoy in an effort to have better sperm. No sauna, no intense exercise, and no alcohol.* He set the bottle down harder than he'd intended to, and the sound clattered through the bar, cutting through the din created by the Friday-night revelers.

Danny walked to the restroom, and Caden tapped Rob on the shoulder. "Are you okay?"

"No, I'm not. Jenny and I have been talking about kids since we met. About how they'd have blue or green eyes and blond hair. How we would teach them to skate and swim. Now there's a strong chance that it will never happen, and I'm standing here listening to Danny whine about being tired because his daughter cries and his son wants attention. I'm not okay, Cade. I'm pissed. Fucking pissed."

Returning from the restroom, Danny clapped Rob on the shoulder as he walked by. "If you need some help in the baby-making, I'm glad to assist. I've always wondered what it would be like with a blonde."

Crack! Rob swung his fist into Danny's mouth, knocking him to the floor.

The people around them scattered as Danny scrambled to his feet and grabbed Rob's shirt. "What the fuck was that?" He swung wildly, and Rob dodged, leaving Danny flailing.

Caden stepped in, separating the two men. The bartender had his phone in his hand, and Caden said, "Don't call the cops. I'll get them out of here. If anything's broken, I'll take care of it." He threw a wad of bills onto the bar. "This should cover the drinks." He grabbed a handful of napkins and grasped both men's arms. "Let's go."

Danny touched his mouth, and his hand came away bloody. "Jesus. I'm bleeding." He reached for Rob, but Caden kept them apart. "You're an asshole."

Rob didn't say a word as Caden led them to the sidewalk.

Caden stood between the two men and pulled out his phone and punched Quinn's number. "Hey, babe. Are you still at the restaurant?" He paused. "I need you to come to O'Malley's stat. Yeah, all three of you. Okay. We're out front." Next, he ordered two Ubers. He handed the napkins to Danny.

"Jesus." Caden swiveled his head between his friends. "We're not in college or on the ice. What were you thinking?" He addressed that to Rob then turned to Danny. "You were out of line. You're drinking yourself stupid."

After a bit, the women came around the corner.

Brooke had the baby in a carrier, and she was the first to speak. "What's going on? Danny, what happened to you?"

"Rob slugged me."

All three women's eyes widened as the first car arrived.

"Quinn, I'm going to ride home with Danny and Brooke so I can take a look at his mouth. There will be another car shortly. Can you ride home with Rob and Jen just to make sure he's okay?" He stepped closer, kissed her hair, and whispered, "I'll explain everything at home."

The second car arrived, and Rob spoke for the first time. "You don't need to come with us, Quinn. Jenny and I don't need a chaperone."

Quinn ignored him and followed them into the car. "Caden asked me to go with you, so I will."

They hadn't gone far when Rob said, "I had too much to drink. Danny was complaining about the kids, and it made me so angry. But the final straw was him saying he'd help us make a baby and how he'd always wanted to be with a blonde. I lost it." He leaned back against the cushions. "Except in a hockey game, I've never thrown a punch in my life."

At their house, Rob sat at the kitchen island while Quinn looked at his bruised hand. "Do you have an ice pack?" she asked Jen. "I mean, obviously, I'm not a doctor, but I don't think it's broken."

Jen opened the freezer. "Of course we do. It gets frequent use after hockey games."

Robbie rested his arms on the island and lowered his head. "I'm sorry, Jenny." His voice was muffled. He looked up and turned his gaze toward Quinn. "Thanks for coming with us. You should head home. I'm okay. Just so fucking angry." He flattened his hand on the counter, and Jenny placed the ice pack on it. "I'll call Cade in the morning." He listened to Quinn talking with Jenny before she left.

"Wanna change your mind about my fathering your kids? Because I'm pretty sure they deserve someone who's not an idiot like me."

Jenny wrapped her arms around him and rested her chin on his head. "Never. You punched a guy for me. That's a first.

175

When you're sober, I'll tell you how that's kinda hot. Let's go to bed."

"Jenny? It wasn't the alcohol. I would have done it stone-cold sober."

Chapter Twenty

My Friends are Falling Apart

Caden

"WELL, THIS IS A big fucking mess." Caden walked through the door, shaking his head.

Quinn was waiting on the couch, and Caden joined her, pulling her legs over his lap. "Rob told us what happened, but I'd like to hear your version," she said.

"He was in a bad place when I got to the bar. He'd already had a couple, and he told me the IUI didn't work."

"Yeah, Jen told us that too. She said they hadn't really processed it together."

Caden nodded and ran his hands along Quinn's legs. "Danny was in a mood when he arrived, and he started pounding down the beer and complaining about everything. It was his moaning about the baby crying and how exhausted they were that got to Rob. Then he made a crack about helping them make a baby."

"That's what Rob told Jen and me."

"That was so far out of line." Caden sighed. "I get why Rob popped him." He snorted. "His fist came out of nowhere, and Danny dropped like a block of cement."

"Is he okay? Relatively speaking."

"I had the car stop here so I could pick up some supplies. When we got to their house, I cleaned the cut and put some butterfly bandages on it. He's still hopping mad, and Brooke is mortified. You know her sister is here?"

Quinn nodded.

"This was an unexpected event for her to witness, and it was clear it embarrassed Brooke." He took a deep breath, exhaled slowly, and ran his hands along Quinn's legs again, eventually letting them drift to her feet.

Quinn looked at him with a questioning smile in her eyes.

Caden smiled back and slid his hands back to her calves. "Later." The smile faded. "My friends are falling apart, Quinn, and I don't know how to help them."

"You talked about an intervention the night Tally was born. Are you still thinking about that? And do you know what it entails?"

"I need to do some research. Does Danny qualify as an alcoholic? Does he need to go to rehab? I don't know the answers."

"My only experience with alcoholism was Sam's dad. It was bad when Sam was a teenager. Trent was emotionally abusive to him and his brothers. Sam knows now that depression played a big role in his dad's behavior. Danny's happy-go-lucky, isn't he? What he said to Rob was a joke." She stared at Caden. "Wasn't it?"

"Not sure happy-go-lucky is how I'd describe Danny. He likes to joke around, but he's also intense. I'm sure he thought he was being funny tonight, but Rob was not in the place to laugh it off." Caden started to massage her feet. "I'm not sure how we're going to come back from this. But enough about that. It's Friday night, and I want to make love to my fiancée."

Quinn had changed into pajama shorts and a robe that he loved. Caden lavished attention first on one foot then the other, smiling at her as she squirmed under his touch. "The first time I saw how a foot massage affected you is one of my favorite memories."

She blushed, as she always did when Caden talked about her enjoyment of having his hands on her feet. She stretched out, and he knew exactly what she wanted.

His hands moved up her legs then came to rest at her center. He teased her, keeping his fingers on the outside of her satin shorts.

"You're overdressed for this party."

Caden stood to remove his shirt and pants. Leaving his boxers on, he stretched out beside her. "Better?"

Quinn's only response was to stroke Caden's obvious bulge while his attention shifted to her breasts. She kissed him, opening her mouth so his tongue could explore. She sighed and whispered, "Are we staying down here?"

"No." But he made no movement toward the bedroom as he enjoyed the comfort of her body against his. "I'm so glad I have you." With one last peck on her lips, he stood and reached for her hand. "Come on. The bed awaits."

"It was good not to be alone last night." Caden and Quinn were sitting at the counter, enjoying coffee and pastries he had ventured out early to buy. "Your two months are almost done."

"Don't remind me."

"Does that mean you'd like to be here permanently?" His phone buzzed. "Hold that thought. This is Rob." He answered, "Hey, how are you doing? You're on speaker. Quinn's here."

"Hey, Quinn. Thanks for looking at my hand last night. I'm suffering a bit this morning. Sore hand, sore head, and feeling like an idiot for letting my emotions get away from me."

"I told Quinn last night I might have reacted the same way."

"No, you wouldn't have. You hardly even fight on the ice."

"You and Jen okay?"

"Yeah." A long pause followed. "We're both disappointed, but we knew it was a long shot. We're going to try again, probably in a couple of weeks, and if it still doesn't work, our next step will be IVF. Have you talked to Danny this morning?"

"No. I butterflied his lip last night. He knew how out of line I thought he was."

"I'm not planning to apologize, Cade. And I won't be back at O'Malley's for a while. I can't take any more of his negativity, and I shouldn't be drinking anyway. We don't want to lose touch with you and Quinn, but prefer it to be the four of us."

"I understand."

"Jenny's going to stay in touch with Brooke, and eventually, I'll make nice with Danny. Just... not right now."

Caden ended the call and stared out the window.

Quinn stood behind him, rubbing his shoulders. "That's hard, huh?"

"It is. But I understand. Last February, after I broke up with you, I stayed away from O'Malley's for two months. I wasn't in the right headspace to be there. It'll work out... hopefully. I still think the drinking needs to be addressed."

"Sam's supposed to call today to tell me how his doctor's visit went. Do you mind if I talk to him about it?"

"No. Please do. I need all the input I can get."

"Do you have any idea how much I'm going to miss this when I go back to New Hampshire?" They were relaxing in the sauna when Quinn's phone rang. "It's Sam. Do you want me to put him on speaker?"

"If you're comfortable doing that."

"Hey, Sam."

Caden listened to her half of the conversation and figured out that Sam had gotten one of his casts off but still had weeks to go for the other. He'd broken his wrist and crushed his ankle in a construction accident earlier in the fall.

Sam must have asked about Caden, because she replied, "He's good. We're sitting in the sauna." After Sam said something else, she continued, "Yup. He does spoil me. Do you mind if I put you on speaker? We want to talk to you about something."

Once she'd done so, Sam said, "Hey, Caden. Kinda strange to be talking to you." During the period that Caden and Quinn were apart, Sam had texted with him.

"Hi, Sam. Glad to hear the wrist is healed. That'll make your life easier." *It's hard to believe I felt threatened by him.*

"So, what do you want to talk about?"

Quinn took the lead in explaining Danny's drinking, with Caden filling in the details.

"He always drank more than Rob and me, but it's grown incrementally since last spring. And he's obnoxious when he's drinking." Caden hated talking about his oldest friend behind his back, but he felt like there was no choice.

"Whooo." Sam blew out a breath. "I know way too much about obnoxious drunks. My dad gave me a thorough education."

"Did the drinking escalate as you and your brothers got older?" Caden was concerned that Danny's drinking would continue to get worse as the kids grew up.

"Yeah. He drank when we were in grade school, and we were afraid of angering him, but it was nothing like it was when we were in high school." Sam paused. "It sucked."

Sam had just given voice to Caden's biggest fear. "Did he stop drinking because friends and family staged an intervention?"

"The only intervention came from my mom. She moved out and told him she wouldn't return while he was drinking."

"But he didn't go to rehab?"

"No, he got sober on his own and eventually went to a therapist for his depression. He's not the same man he was when I was a teenager. Does Danny think it's a problem?"

"That's the burning question." Caden sighed. "And I don't have an answer."

"I was drinking a lot a year ago, and I knew it was trouble. When I had Piper, I was fine, but not when I was alone. Therapy made all the difference for me." Sam snorted. "Quinn, it was that night you picked me up at the Sidecar that did it. When you told me I was nothing but a drunk, and I realized how badly I'd behaved."

Quinn rolled her eyes and gripped Caden's hand. "Not the finest night for either of us."

"I don't know if this will make sense to you, but it's something I've thought about. My dad lost my mom because of his drinking, and he stopped because it was the only way to get her back. I lost nothing because of my drinking. It wasn't the reason Norah moved out, and it wasn't why things didn't work out with you, Quinn. I drank because *I* was lost. I stopped because I didn't like who I had become. Everyone has different motivations."

"What about now? Does your dad drink at all?" Caden asked. "And do you?"

"If he does, he's hiding it very well. I limit myself to one drink, and I openly admit I'm a work in progress. I fell off the wagon last summer. Ironically, my dad came to see me and told me he hoped my brothers and I hadn't inherited his drinking problem. That got me on the right track again."

"I appreciate your openness."

"No problem. I hope it helps."

After Sam hung up, Quinn asked, "What do you think?"

Caden shook his head. "I don't know. I think a lot is going to depend on Brooke and how big a problem she thinks it is."

Chapter Twenty-One

New Year, New Plan

Jenny

JEN WALKED INTO DR. Kerr's office the week after New Year's. Robbie had texted her he'd be about fifteen minutes late and went over the top apologizing, but she knew it wouldn't be a problem with the doctors. They were so kind and understanding. The second IUI had failed, and they had decided to try IVF. They'd done research on their own, and Jen hoped the picture she had in mind was more accurate than the one she'd had for IUI.

They'd skipped the New Year's Eve party for the first time since they met. Quinn and Caden spent the holiday in New

Hampshire, and Robbie still hadn't seen Danny since the night in November when he had hit him. Danny would be traveling with the Patriots, leaving Brooke home with the kids.

Robbie had surprised Jenny with a weekend in Montreal. It was the first time they'd been out of Boston since their trip to the lake. He'd rented a Land Rover for the drive. They stayed in a luxury hotel, ate delicious food, and watched fireworks at midnight. Jenny hoped the new year would be a fresh start, that friendships would be repaired, and by the next New Year's Eve, they would be celebrating with their baby.

"Hey, darlin'. Sorry I'm late." The new year had brought a calm to Robbie. He had come to terms with his low sperm count, and when they were in Montreal, they'd discussed what they would do if IVF failed. He leaned in to kiss her then sank into a chair. "We've got a new client in Chicago. I may have to travel there, but I made it clear where my priorities are." In September, he would not have admitted to his colleagues that they were doing IVF.

"We'll figure it out." Jenny squeezed his hand just as Jed came to the meeting room.

"Ivy is under the weather, so you're stuck with me." He took them to the conference room. "She and I reviewed your case last week and have a plan mapped out. We did all the preliminary exams last fall. Your periods are regular, you're already taking the suggested supplements, and you've made the lifestyle modifications. So if you're ready, we can start right in with the main act."

Robbie winked at Jenny.

Her stomach did a somersault. She was happy to have the old Robbie back and excited to be starting the process. "We're ready."

"I thought you were. The hormone injections will start on the second day of your period. That should be around ten days from now. Are you going to do those yourself, Jen?"

Robbie answered, "No, I'll do it."

"We have a video you can watch, and you'll have an appointment where you learn to mix the medications and administer them. You'll come in on day two of your cycle for a baseline appointment where we'll do bloodwork and an ultrasound. If everything looks good, you'll start the injections that day. It's going to be two shots for the first six days, then a third will be added. You'll come in every two days for blood tests and ultrasounds to check on the follicle growth and numbers. Any questions about that part of the process?"

They both shook their heads.

"You may experience some side effects. You have the paperwork that outlines all of that. If there is ever anything going on that you have questions about, call the office immediately. You can set up your appointments on the way out." He smiled at them. "Enjoy the next ten days. It's going to be intense once you start the injections."

Eleven days later, Jenny and Robbie walked into the doctor's office. Jenny had a death grip on Robbie's hand. "I have such butterflies."

"I know. Me too."

Earlier in the week, they were shown how to mix the medications, and Robbie learned how to do the injections.

After the lab work and ultrasound, Ivy entered the exam room. "Everything looks good. If you're ready, it's go time. Remember to do the injections at the same time every day, and we'll see you in two days to see if we need to make any adjustments."

At home, Robbie rubbed an ice cube over the injection site and took a deep breath.

Jenny was breathing steadily and looking away. "Don't hesitate. Be decisive. And don't tell me it's coming because I'll tense up. Just do it."

She felt the prick and heard Robbie blow out a breath.

"One down, one to go. How'd I do?"

"Not bad. It was like a mosquito bite."

He did the second shot, and Jenny inhaled several times and exhaled with a pained expression.

"Bad? Was it me?"

Trying to breathe through the pain, she said, "I don't think it was you. The paperwork said it would burn. Hold me?"

Robbie sat on the bed and wrapped his arms around her. "I hate that I'm hurting you."

"I'll be okay. It's subsiding." She relaxed in his arms. "Just ten more days."

The next morning, he brought her coffee. "You didn't sleep well. I felt you tossing and turning."

"I had weird dreams." She pushed up to a sitting position and took a sip of the coffee. "My boobs hurt."

The next day, they had another doctor's visit with lab work and an ultrasound.

Ivy met them with a smile. "Everything looks exactly as we want it to. How are you tolerating the injections? Are you having any side effects?"

"The second shot really burns, and my breasts are killing me. More than anything I've ever had with my period."

"We're flooding your body with a lot of hormones. Sometimes, the side effects subside as time goes on."

"But not every time?"

"Sadly, no."

On the third morning, Jenny took a swallow of the coffee Robbie brought her and immediately jumped out of bed to run to the bathroom, where she heaved it up. The weird dreams continued, although she couldn't remember any details when she awoke. Later that morning, she snapped at her personal assistant.

Seven days in, the side effects had not abated. The day before, the third shot had been added, and it burned more than the others. Robbie held her every night while she lay with the heating pad on her abdomen. *I've tried to keep how terrible I feel from him, but I know I'm failing.*

While Robbie was working out with Caden, Jenny took a bath, hoping that would ease the ache in her breasts. She sank under the water up to her chin, resting her hands on her abdomen. It was distended, and the day before, she'd struggled to zip her jeans. But the mood swings were the worst. People at work were tiptoeing around her, afraid of invoking her wrath. She'd met Brooke for lunch and cried as she held Tally. *I had no idea my body could feel this bad or that I'd be so out of control emotionally.*

It was taking everything she had to hide her emotions from Robbie. But he saw the physical effects every day. Those were impossible to hide. No matter what Jen ate in the morning, it came back up. Her breasts were swollen and heavy. She shook her head. Normally, bigger boobs would have been something Robbie teased her about, but he knew how uncomfortable she was, and there was no joking.

She stepped out of the tub and toweled off then stood in front of the mirror. She ran her hands over her abdomen and up to her breasts. They still ached. Her hands went back to her stomach. *Only a few more days. It's all going to be worth it because in a few months, this will be a baby bump.*

Jenny lay on the exam table with Robbie holding her hand, as he always did. The tech had just completed the transvaginal ultrasound, and Jenny should have been getting dressed, but lying down felt too good. Exhaustion had hit her that morning, and she had struggled to make it through the workday. "I should have stayed home today. I was falling asleep at my desk."

When Ivy walked in, Jenny knew from her expression that she was surprised to see her still supine on the exam table. "I'm too tired to move."

"I have good news for you. You have ten follicles, and they're eighteen millimeters, so you're ready for the trigger shot. That should be done at ten tonight. We'll see you back here the day after tomorrow at eight for the retrieval."

Jenny listened to Robbie getting dressed in the bathroom. *I should get up, but I can't.* She'd been drifting in and out of sleep since he'd left the bed. The thought of putting clothes on was too much. The sheets were soft on her skin, leaving her feeling the best she had in days. She fumbled on the nightstand for her phone and sent a brief text to her assistant to let her know she was going to take the day off and would be back in the office on Monday. Then she drifted back to sleep with the phone in her hand.

When Robbie lifted the phone, her eyes popped open. "I'm staying home today."

"That's a good idea. Can I get you some breakfast?"

"I don't want to risk it. I just want to sleep."

Robbie came back with a jug of water. "You have to stay hydrated, and tonight you have to eat dinner."

"I know." She burrowed under the covers.

That night, after drinking all the water and picking at the chicken and rice Robbie cooked, Jenny sat enveloped in his arms and began to cry.

"Darlin', we're close to the finish line. Now's not the time to cry." It was the first time she had cried in front of him.

"I don't even know why I'm crying. I'm just on edge all the time."

"All the time? Have you been hiding that from me?"

"Yes." She hiccupped. "I don't want to make you feel worse."

"Lie down." He arranged the pillows so she could lie on her side then rubbed her back while he talked. "I know you feel like crap. You can't hide that, but is it also your emotions? I thought maybe we'd escaped that one."

"No. You should see my colleagues. They don't even want to talk to me for fear I'll bite their heads off."

"You're trying to protect me because you know how guilty I feel about you having to go through this. And I've been trying to stay upbeat so you won't worry about me. We're a pair." He leaned forward to kiss her hair. "We need to keep reminding ourselves that we'll be honest about our feelings."

The next morning, Robbie had to provide the sample on his own since Jen was sedated for the egg retrieval. When he was done, he rejoined Jenny, who had awoken and was eating some crackers.

Jed came in to talk with them. "We got four eggs."

Jenny's heart sank. *All this for only four eggs.* Tears welled in her eyes.

"I know you were hoping for more than that, and so were we. Remember, it only takes one fertilized egg to grow into an embryo. We're going to inject a sperm into each egg, then we'll see what happens. We'll call you in the morning to let you know if any of the eggs are fertilized."

On Sunday morning, Jen's phone pinged. She showed the screen to Robbie. "Hi, Jed. You're on speaker."

"Hi, Jen. Hi, Robbie. We've got one fertilized egg. Again, not as many as we were hoping for, but it's not unusual. We'll see you on Tuesday, and if everything has gone the way we want it to, we'll proceed with the transfer. If it hasn't, we'll have a discussion as to why and discuss our next steps."

Jenny knew the minute she saw Jed's face on Tuesday afternoon.

"Unfortunately, the fertilized egg did not continue to divide. I'm sorry."

Robbie turned and wrapped his arms around Jenny. "Do you know why?" he asked while she silently wept.

"There could be several reasons. We suspect the eggs were immature."

"Did we harvest them too soon?" Jenny raised her head from Robbie's shoulder and dabbed at her eyes with a tissue.

"Not necessarily, but we will change the protocol slightly for the next round."

"Will we start when I have my period?"

"Let's wait one cycle. Your body needs some time to recover, and you both need to heal emotionally. Your period should start in the next ten to fourteen days, then we'll try again with the period after that."

Chapter Twenty-Two

Quinn's Decision

Quinn

QUINN CONTEMPLATED THE GLASS of wine in front of her. She'd spent October and November living with Caden and working at Mass General. Then she'd returned to Dartmouth for the past two months, and they had resumed commuting between Hanover and Boston. She smiled as she thought of Cade telling her he wished there were such a thing as frequent-driver miles. She was in Boston for the weekend, and on Sunday, Caden would follow her back to Hanover and stay for February and March while he worked at Dartmouth. Her time in Boston had been everything she'd hoped for, and in her heart, she knew she'd be giving up her job in New Hampshire to relocate to Boston permanently.

But it would be fun having Caden with her in New Hampshire before making the big move. He would get to know her friends better and work in a different environment. She treasured his friends, but her tribe, which she'd grown when she settled in Hanover and sworn off men, would always have a place in her heart. Caden's sister Claire had told her she could stay in the guesthouse whenever she wanted to visit. That was where she and Caden had made love for the first time, and she adored the quirky structure, which she thought of as an overgrown dollhouse.

Caden was having his last Friday night at O'Malley's for a couple of months, and Rob was joining him and Danny for the first time since the fight just before Thanksgiving. Butterflies fluttered in Quinn's stomach, partly because she knew how anxious Caden was about it.

Brooke interrupted Quinn's thoughts when she pulled a chair away from the table and slid into it. "I've missed you," she said. "And good grief, it's going to be two months before I see you again."

"You could always come north for a weekend."

"Maybe I will. It might be good to get out of the city. And I could see that guesthouse of Claire's that you keep raving about."

Jen joined them and immediately ordered a glass of Chablis. "Since I'm not pregnant, I might as well indulge. Sorry you can't join us, Brooke."

Quinn tried to read Jen's mood. She knew they had gotten no viable embryos from their first try at IVF, and she had expected her friend to be sad. But that wasn't quite what she was showing.

"It won't be too long. Nursing may end soon."

"You nursed Liam until he was almost a year old."

"He was older when I went back to work, and... things were different." Brooke had returned to work three weeks earlier, after the Patriots' season had ended. Her interior design business operated out of a small studio on Newbury Street.

Quinn knew the story. A year ago, Brooke had been thinking about taking on an associate. She'd realized she was pregnant in February and started working on a business plan for expansion. If she had another designer working with her, she'd be able to be away longer when the baby was born then work part-time for a while. She had planned on bringing someone on in June. Then in March, Danny had been passed over for a job promotion, and he was devastated.

Brooke had thought they could weather it. They'd been through other challenges, and the ship always righted itself. But March turned into April and April into May. Danny was drinking more heavily than Brooke had seen since they were in college. He had days he didn't get out of bed, and any help around the house became nonexistent. She had chosen June as the month to bring someone on board because it was a slower time for him, and she thought he would pick up the slack with Liam and around the house while she worked more hours to make sure the expansion went smoothly. Her intention had been to interview designers in May. By the middle of the month, she'd known her plan wouldn't work, and she reluctantly shelved it.

Soon after Quinn had returned from Honduras, she and Brooke met for lunch, and Quinn innocently asked how the expansion had gone. Brooke had spilled all the details, ending by saying, "Our life fell apart just as yours with Caden did. You've worked things out. Hopefully, Danny and I will too."

Quinn had been embarrassed that Caden hadn't told her more about Danny and Brooke's struggles, but when they reunited in Honduras, their only focus had been on each other. Then she discovered that because Caden had isolated himself before he went to Honduras, he was unaware of how badly Danny had fallen apart.

Brooke's distress over Danny's drinking had been obvious as she went through the last month of her pregnancy. Quinn thought about the night Tally was born then about how Rob had slugged Danny. After the tough months when she and Caden were apart, she was gloriously happy with her life, but her heart ached for her friends. She reached her hand across the table to Brooke's arm. "I'm sorry."

Brooke shrugged. "I thought Danny would take over the morning duties. You know, getting the kids to daycare or maybe even, God forbid, keeping them home with him. All I'd have to do was nurse Tally before I left and make sure I'd pumped enough to last the day." She rubbed her forehead. "It's been three weeks, and that hasn't happened. I'm frustrated and worn out. If I switch Tally to formula, it will take the nursing and pumping time off my plate." After a pause, she said, "I'm so sorry, Jen. I know how much you want a baby and all that goes with it, and here I am, being Negative Nellie."

Jen slid over to hug her. "Don't worry. I won't hit you."

Both women chuckled sadly. They'd discussed the incident at O'Malley's and agreed that no matter what was going on between their husbands, they would not let it affect their friendship.

Quinn wrapped her arms around them. "That's why we get together. So we can say all the things we can't say to our partners. I have that with my tribe in New Hampshire. We cook a meal once a month, and let me tell you, it's easy to let everything out while you're chopping onions or peeling potatoes. I was the only single one in the group, and boy, the complaints I used to hear about husbands. I want to have that with you two."

Brooke grinned. "I'm never going to believe you have any criticism of Cade."

"Not right at the moment." Quinn blushed. "Things are pretty fantastic." Part of her hated being so happy when Brooke and Jen were suffering.

As if Jen could read her mind, she said, "And don't you dare feel bad about feeling good. Everything will work out for us."

"Ever the optimist," Brooke muttered. "How are you?"

"Sad." Tears welled in her eyes. "Just sad. Robbie and I both are." Jen took a deep breath. "But I'm so relieved to be off the hormones. Today is the first day that I'm feeling slightly more like myself."

"The side effects were bad?" Quinn hadn't seen her while she was getting the injections. "I've had two friends who did IVF. One of them sailed through easily, and the other had a harder time."

"It was terrible. My whole body ached, and I was bloated and bitchy. I kept reminding myself to focus on the prize, but it was a struggle."

"Are you going to try again?"

"Yes, but not until the cycle after this. They told me to let my body recover. I had such a mixture of emotions that day with the doctor. Such disappointment because we didn't get any embryos but also overwhelming relief at stopping the hormones. Am I going to feel that bad if I get pregnant?"

Quinn and Brooke both shrugged.

Brooke answered, "I'm a bad one to ask because other than all-day morning sickness for a couple of months, I felt fine." She turned to Quinn. "Remember when we mentioned a third right after Tally's birth?"

Quinn nodded.

"We said that because both pregnancies had been relatively easy. But now? That's not happening unless there's a drastic improvement between Danny and me."

"I've read about women who have done several IVF cycles. I don't think I can do that, and I don't know how to tell Robbie."

"He'll understand."

"He will, but it will be one more thing that he will internalize as being his fault. It's hard. We've promised to be open. But we still try to shield each other. We hide things that will make them sad." She waved a hand. "We're a mess, and we won't fix that tonight. Let's find happier subjects. Do you have any interesting projects, Brooke?"

"I thought I would ease my way back with a few minor jobs, and I have those. But I've also taken on an enormous one. Quinn, did you meet Trinity Gammish when you were working here?"

"Is she the new doctor who's in charge of the neurology department? We had dinner with her one night."

"That's her. She was the chief resident when Cade started med school. After she completed her residency, she pursued a fellowship in Los Angeles and remained there for a few years. Now she's back and has bought the top floor of the new building going up on Necco Street."

"The whole top floor?" Quinn shook her head in disbelief. Her new acquaintances had money that blew her away. Then she laughed. "I love that there is a street named after Necco Wafers."

Brooke and Jen laughed with her before Brooke answered, "Yup. The penthouse. It's a blank canvas, and she wants me to do the whole thing. She saw Caden's brownstone and liked my work."

"That's outstanding."

"No, what it really is, is overwhelming. But I'm excited."

"How big is the 'whole top floor'?"

"Over five thousand square feet. I'll be working on it until early summer. She seems very nice, one of those dream clients. Kinda like Cade was." Brooke's face was flushed. "Your turn, Quinn. Any wedding plans?"

"The wedding is going to be in July on Caden's rooftop terrace."

"I love that." Jen clapped her hands. "But it means not many people."

"Yes. Just immediate family and close friends. You guys, obviously, and a few people from Hanover. We'll be working on the plans while Cade's living with me. You don't need to tell me it will be drastically different from the wedding Caden was going to have with Mary."

"It will be. But much truer to Cade. That extravaganza was all driven by Mary." Brooke smiled. "I can't wait to see what you do up there."

"And for a spot to live?" Jen asked.

Neither Jen nor Brooke wanted to see Caden leave Boston, but they knew he was considering it.

"I loved my two months here in the fall." Quinn paused, leaving her friends to wonder if there was a *but* coming. "Unless Caden decides he enjoys being crammed into my little two-bedroom townhouse, which lacks a gym and a sauna, I'll be moving to Boston."

"That's the best news." Brooke put her hand on the table, and the two other women piled theirs on top of hers. "How do you think the boys are getting along?"

Chapter Twenty-Three

Success!

Robbie

ROBBIE LEANED BACK AT his desk. A month and a half had passed since they'd gotten the crushing news that their first try at IVF had not produced one viable embryo. Jenny's second period since then had started two days ago, and later today, they would go back to see Jed and Ivy. Then the injections would start again. He shook his head, trying to dislodge the vision of how miserable Jenny had been while she was receiving the hormones. *The thought of going through this entire process again just kills me. If our results are as poor this time, I'm going to push for us to use donor sperm.*

They had discussed it briefly, way back in the fall, but agreed they wanted their child to share their DNA. Robbie had reached the point where he didn't care. He wanted Jenny to carry their child, and it was looking less and less like that was going to happen with his sperm. When he was still processing the news that he was sterile, piling on the idea of some other guy's seed impregnating Jenny was unthinkable. *If I've learned anything since September, and I've learned a lot, it's to check my ego at the door.*

"Hey, darlin'," Robbie greeted Jenny outside the doctor's office, determined to keep the atmosphere light.

A pinched expression crossed her face as she gave him a quick hug. "They're going to change the protocol, and I'm nervous that I'll feel even worse this time."

When they met with Jed and Ivy, just as Jenny suspected, Ivy said, "We're going to try a different combination this time. The aim is for more follicles and, more importantly, more mature eggs."

"Should I expect the same side effects? Or worse?"

"It's hard to say. I hope not."

Jed added, "There is one change we want you to implement. Rob, we want you to ejaculate on day seven. We understand you may not feel like having intercourse, Jen, so masturbation is fine. We expect to do the retrieval on day twelve, so that will put your sample at the optimal time."

A week later, Robbie returned from a workout to find Jenny soaking in the tub. The protocol had started with three shots, and they had added a fourth on the night before. She told him that so far, the side effects had not been as bad. She'd been nauseated on the second day and again the last two, but she hadn't vomited. He watched as she ran her hands over her breasts, then they drifted to her belly. Thankfully, she wasn't experiencing negative mood swings. Jenny told him she'd had periods of excitement but none of the rage.

She climbed out of the tub, and he was waiting with a towel. "How are you doing?" The question had become more than a generic greeting between them, and Jenny seemed glad to respond positively. "I'm well. Really well."

He grinned at her. "That's good to hear. I need a shower."

"I'll be in bed, waiting." She grinned back at him.

After Robbie was done, he lifted the blanket and was surprised to find Jenny naked. "What's going on, darlin'?"

"We have a job to do." She spread her hands. "It's day seven. Remember?"

"I do. But figured it would be a solitary pursuit."

He'd put boxers on after his shower, and Jenny stroked his middle. "I feel good. Much better than last time. It may not last, so let's take advantage." She grabbed his hand and brought it to her breast. "I mean, have you noticed these boobs?"

"I have, but I didn't think you'd want me to touch."

"Try. I'll tell you if it's too much."

Robbie brought his lips to hers, and Jenny opened her mouth. His tongue knocked against her teeth, and he wrapped his arms around her, bringing their bodies together. He was gentle, and when the fit between them was different, he looked at her quizzically.

"I'm bloated."

"Okay. Are you uncomfortable?"

"I'm the opposite of uncomfortable right now." She giggled.

Robbie's face burst into a broad smile. "Is this like a tiny preview of what a baby bump will feel like?"

"I think so."

He continued to hold her, rubbing circles on her back while they adjusted to the new fit. "It's subtle. But I know you so well. You've felt the same way against me since our first time."

"I know. Robbie?"

He cocked his head.

"It feels really good to be close to you like this."

"Mmmm." His hand wandered to her breast, and he fondled it tenderly.

Jenny squirmed. "That feels good." She snaked her hand between them, searching for his growing erection. When she found it, Robbie groaned as her fingers teased him. "You might want to take these boxers off."

"I might." Robbie chuckled as he stood and shoved his underwear to the floor. Then he pulled the blanket down again and drank in the sight of Jenny. She was on her back, and he sat beside her. He bent to kiss her then fluttered kisses down her neck to her breast and ran his tongue over the nipple, savoring her response.

Jenny lay quietly as his erection grew. She reached for it and stroked from balls to tip.

Robbie straightened and replaced his tongue with his hands. He enjoyed the subtle increase in size before moving his hands over her belly to between her legs. She was wet, and he teased her clit then slipped a finger inside.

She squirmed against his hand and increased her pressure on his erection.

"We don't have to do this. I'm okay with your hand or mine."

"Robbie. Have you lost your mind? Do I seem like I don't want to do it?"

"No. But..."

In response, Jenny spread her legs. "Take me. Please."

He climbed on top of her and eased his cock in. When she'd taken him completely, he kept his hips still and brought his lips to hers. Resting his weight on his forearms, he gazed into her eyes. "Do you know how much I love you?"

"As much as I love you." She thrust against him. "I wasn't sure I'd ever be horny again."

Robbie shifted. "I was a little worried about that too."

They moved together slowly at first then faster as desire grew. Robbie came first, and when Jenny's orgasm was slow to happen, his fingers found her clit. His touch nudged her over the edge, and they collapsed against each other.

As their breathing slowed, Jenny pulled the blanket over them and settled against Robbie. "Are your hopes up? Because I'll be honest. My hopes are up."

"Yeah. I'm having a hard time tempering my expectations. Not long now."

Jen was nauseated again the next morning and barely made it through her workday. When Robbie gave her the injections that night, she cried. He held her while she tried to find comfort from the heating pad.

"Is this because of what we did last night?"

Jenny shook her head. "I think my body has just had enough."

When it was time for the trigger shot, she felt as miserable as she had during the first cycle.

After the retrieval, Ivy joined them, smiling broadly. "You had fifteen follicles at twenty millimeters, and we got ten eggs. This is an excellent result."

Jenny squeezed Robbie's hand, and they were almost giddy as they made their way home.

They waited with bated breath for the call the next day, which told them six eggs had fertilized.

Again, they waited with bated breath until their appointment two days later, where they found out that four of the eggs had progressed to embryos.

"Does that mean we do the transfer today?" Jenny smiled at Robbie and clutched his hand while waiting for Jed's answer.

"Yes. We prefer to do transfers on the third day. We believe in returning the embryo to its natural environment as early as possible. The other embryos will be monitored, and if they continue to develop, we will freeze them on day five, as we discussed."

Ivy entered the room as Jed finished talking. Smiling, she asked, "Are you ready to get pregnant?"

Jenny nodded enthusiastically.

Robbie asked, "Can I stay while you do it?"

"Absolutely. It's a much simpler procedure than the retrieval was." She handed Jen a quart of water. "Drink this over the next ten to fifteen minutes then relax for an hour, and we'll be back."

Jenny leaned against Robbie on the couch. "I'm going to be pregnant. Can you believe it?"

Holding her, he rested his chin on her head. "You've done all the hard parts. You deserve this."

"No, *we* deserve it." She took his hand and placed it over her heart. "Can you feel that? My heart is beating so fast."

"I know. Mine is too."

When the transfer was completed, Ivy gave them a few minutes to relax then returned to the exam room. "We want you to continue the progesterone injections."

Jenny groaned. Those were her least favorite of the shots Robbie gave her every night.

"I know. They're uncomfortable, but progesterone serves so many purposes, and it's very necessary. If everything goes as we hope, we'll start tapering it around eight weeks."

"I know I'm being a baby. Thanks for reminding me how important it is."

"One last thing. You're going to want to take a pregnancy test. We recommend waiting until day twelve, and if you can't make it that long, at least wait until day ten. Implantation will happen between day six and day twelve, and you won't have a positive test until then." Ivy smiled. "Do you want a call letting you know how the remaining embryos have progressed, or do you want to find out when you come to confirm the pregnancy?"

Robbie answered, "We'd like a call."

Jenny clutched Robbie's hand as they left the building. "I have *our* baby inside me. I didn't think this was ever going to happen."

Robbie pulled her close to him. "It's exciting. But you're not officially pregnant, are you?"

"Way to burst my bubble." She frowned at him in mock anger. "I know there's no guarantee that it will implant. But I am excited. Are you?"

"I am so excited, Jenny. I will have every appendage crossed for luck until you take that pregnancy test."

"Me too."

Two days later, Jed called to tell them that none of the embryos had continued to develop. Robbie held Jenny as she cried. *It's my crappy sperm. What are we going to do if she's not pregnant?*

On day nine, Jenny came home with three pregnancy tests and placed them on the counter. "This is killing me. I can't wait three more days."

"How about if you take it not tomorrow but the day after?" Robbie wanted to know as much as she did, but he was terrified of getting negative results.

She sighed but agreed to wait.

The next night, they both slept fitfully, and at six in the morning, she nudged Robbie. "Come on. We said we'd do it today, and I need to pee."

She placed the stick on the sink and turned away. "I can't look."

"Don't we need to wait three minutes?"

Jenny nodded and tapped her hands against her thighs, trying to quell her nerves.

Robbie was tracking the time on his watch, and at two minutes, he leaned over to look. "Babe," he breathed. "There're two lines."

She grabbed the stick to look at it then threw her arms around him. "We did it! We're having a baby!" She laughed as Robbie held her. "Oh my God. I can't believe we actually did it."

The next day, Jenny had blood drawn to establish a baseline hCG level. She returned two days later, and the number had doubled.

Ivy gave them the results. "This is exactly what we want to see. We want you to come in every two days so we can continue to monitor the hCG for a week or two, but I'm thrilled with these results."

The number continued to rise, and after a week, Jenny told Robbie he didn't need to go with her. "They're just going to draw blood, and I'm going to sit around waiting for the results. I can do it on my own. Really."

After two more blood tests, she was told she didn't need to come back for ten days.

That night, after the progesterone injection, Robbie held her as she tried to get comfortable.

"I was sick this morning after you left."

"More than just nauseated?" The nausea that started plaguing her before the transfer had been getting worse.

"Oh yeah. I totally lost my breakfast."

"I'm sorry." He rubbed her shoulders. "I spent my morning researching what our little miracle looks like right now." He showed her the screenshots.

"They'll do an ultrasound at the next appointment. It won't look like much, but we'll hear the heartbeat."

"I can't wait for that."

When that day came, Jed moved the wand, and a rapid whooshing sound came through the speakers. "There we go. That's a good heartbeat for this early." He smiled at Jenny and Robbie, who both had tears in their eyes. Jed finished the exam and gave them a few minutes alone.

As Jenny dressed, she said, "That was our baby. Can you believe it?"

Robbie wrapped his arms around her, experiencing her warmth, knowing the baby they'd worked so hard for was growing inside her. He couldn't contain the tears that flowed down his cheeks. "You have my whole heart, Jenny."

Chapter Twenty-Four

Devestation

Caden

CADEN SPENT AN HOUR moving clothes around in his closet. It was the end of May, and the next day would be Quinn's last one working at Dartmouth. She had plans for dinner with her girlfriends, and on Saturday, she would begin moving her stuff to Boston. Her new job would start after their honeymoon. Caden had paid off the mortgage on her townhouse, and they were still deciding what to do with it.

The spring night was warm, and Caden took a beer out to the terrace off the living room. He remembered sitting there a year ago, before his trip to Honduras, and marveled at how his life had changed. In less than two months, he would marry Quinn. They had nearly all the pieces for the wedding in place. The night before, they found the answer to the biggest question. He'd been unable to decide on a best man. When Danny and Brooke got married, Caden had played that role, and for years, he'd thought Danny would stand up with him. But his friendship with Rob had grown stronger over the past year, and Danny had become someone he barely recognized. No matter which of them he chose, the other would be hurt, and Caden didn't want to do that.

Quinn had not selected a maid of honor, either, as she was trying to decide between Ashley and Izzy. Finally, the previous night, they had agreed to forgo having anyone stand up with them. They would enter the rooftop terrace together after their guests had arrived. Quinn loved her father dearly, but at thirty years old, she didn't feel the need to have anyone give her away, and her dad was fine with that. Her parents and Caden's would greet the guests prior to the ceremony.

Caden stretched his legs, happy that the wedding details were coming together. They'd also started working on the foundation. Figuring that out would be easier with Quinn in Boston full time. They had done so much traveling between their homes that time for other things had been short.

His thoughts veered back to his friends. Rob had returned to O'Malley's at the end of January, and there was an uneasy truce between him and Danny. Neither of them had apologized, and the Friday-night gatherings had been few. Caden was in Hanover for February and March and had missed some Friday nights since he returned to Boston. When he saw Danny at the bar, he seemed to have his drinking under control, but he knew from Brooke that he was still a mess. She told him there were days Danny didn't get out of bed, and he wasn't giving her nearly enough help with Liam and Tally.

Rob had shared nothing else about his and Jen's efforts to have a baby, but he suspected that something might be up because Rob had been much more relaxed the last time Caden saw him.

His phone rang, and Caden smiled, certain it was Quinn calling. But to his surprise, Brooke was on the other end.

"Hey, Brooke. What's up?"

"I don't know where Danny is. He's not answering my calls or texts."

Caden checked the time. It was nearly eleven. "How long since you've heard from him?"

"He stormed out after the kids went to bed. Between eight and nine." Her voice held a hint of panic that Caden rarely heard from her. "I called O'Malley's, and he's not there. I'm sorry to bother you, but can you call him? Maybe he'll answer you."

"I'll call, and if he doesn't answer, I know a couple of places I can check. I'll find him, Brooke."

Dammit, Danny, where are you? When his messages went unanswered, Caden changed into jeans and thought about where his friend might be.

O'Malley's was his first stop because it was close, and the bartender might have lied to Brooke. Danny wasn't there, but Caden found out he had been earlier.

The Tavern came next, but no one there had seen him. Caden stood on the sidewalk, trying to get into Danny's head, which wasn't as easy as it had once been.

He headed toward the waterfront and ducked into a couple of bars with no success.

Finally, he found himself in front of Tito's, a dive they had frequented in college, and Caden guessed he hadn't been there in over ten years. He pushed open the door, and memories washed over him. The smell was familiar, the floor was as sticky as Caden remembered, and at the bar, talking with a woman, was a man with a familiar head of red hair. *What the fuck is he doing?*

Caden sidled up to his friend. "What's up, Dan?" He was sure the woman Danny was talking to must be using a fake ID, because she didn't look any older than eighteen.

"Hey, Cade. I didn't expect to run into you here. Let me guess. Brooke sent you."

"She called. She's concerned. I figured out where you were on my own." Danny was obviously not happy to see him, but he wasn't as drunk as Caden had expected. "You should go home."

"No."

"What?"

"I'm not going home."

The woman he'd been talking to backed away from the bar. "You've got something going on. I'm leaving."

Caden was happy to watch her walk away. He turned his attention back to Danny. "Where are you going if not home?"

Danny shrugged. "Don't know."

Caden looked around the bar. "Come home with me."

Danny studied him for several moments then finally said, "Okay."

They walked silently from the waterfront to the Back Bay, and when they reached Caden's brownstone, Danny flopped onto the couch. "I'm not drunk."

"I believe you." Caden handed him a bottle of water and sat in the chair across from him. "What's going on?"

"What did Brooke tell you?"

"Just that she didn't know where you were and you weren't answering her calls."

Danny snorted. "We had a fight. A big fight. I don't want Liam to hear that kind of thing. Thank God Tally's too young." He took a long swallow from the bottle. "She's fucking around on me, Cade."

"Danny. She wouldn't do that."

"Take a guess how long it's been since we had sex."

Caden raised his hands. "I have no idea."

"Since she found out she was pregnant with Tally. Well over a year. We've never gone that long. She's getting it somewhere else."

"Are you?"

"No! I wouldn't do that."

"What were you doing at Tito's?"

"She was a kid. I won't fuck around with a kid. I was having a beer, and she started talking to me."

"Danny, you've been a mess since last spring. I know I checked out on you, and then I was gone, but I'm here now. You've made no effort to tell me what's going on."

"You got pretty judgy at the hospital when Tally was born."

"Your wife was in labor! And you were drinking. Yeah, I had a problem with that."

"I don't like fighting with you. Or with Rob. I know I was out of line last fall, and I'm working to do better."

"Are you really?"

"Yeah. Is Brooke talking shit about me?"

"She told Quinn and Jennifer that you're not going to work, spending all day in bed, and not helping with the kids."

Danny finished the water, went to the kitchen, and got another one. When he sat back on the couch, he laser focused on Caden. "I quit my job today."

"Quit or got fired?"

"Quit." Danny shook his head. "I've been doing my job. You know how it works. We work every day from preseason through the Super Bowl. And at this time of year, unless there's something big going on, we split our time, working anywhere from two to four days a week. I haven't been skipping work, even though I've been miserable."

Quinn's cat, Max, jumped into Danny's lap and nuzzled his chest, insisting on being petted.

Danny dug his fingers into Max's orange fur. "I can't believe Brooke is painting me that way." He focused on Caden again. "Or that you'd believe it."

"Maybe I misunderstood. It was secondhand. You know how that goes."

"Yeah. I could do more with the kids. But the rest..." He shook his head.

"Is that what the fight was about? You quitting?"

"I haven't even told her."

Caden's kitten joined Max on Danny's lap, demanding pets.

Danny laughed as he petted the small gray cat. "You've got a damn menagerie here."

After a few minutes of attention to the cats, he said, "She went at me about getting home late, not helping with the kids, and it disintegrated from there. And I left."

"I'm going to let her know you're staying here tonight," Caden said as he started texting.

Danny shrugged.

"Do you have another job lined up?"

"Possibly. You know Arnie?"

222

"Your old boss?"

"Yeah, the one who recommended me for his job when he left, for all the good that did. He moved to the White Mountains and started a public relations firm. He wants to expand, and he's offered me a job."

"Are you going to leave the city?"

"I can work remotely. But honestly, I don't know." He rubbed his jaw. "Did Brooke answer?"

"She's glad you're safe."

"I can't go on like this."

The next morning, as Caden released his third patient, he thought about the conversation with Danny. It had gone better than any they'd had in more than a year. Danny got up when Cade did and asked if he could stay one more night. *Could Brooke be cheating?* That would be totally out of character. *But so is the idea of them going a year without sex.* He thought about the time he'd shared an apartment with Danny and how active he and Brooke were. And Danny wasn't shy about letting Caden know that had continued after they married.

The morning was quieter than usual, and Caden was thinking about lunch when a nurse tapped him on the shoulder. "We've got a thirty-three-year-old woman in cubicle four. Probable miscarriage."

"Okay." Caden ran a hand through his hair. Lunch would have to wait. He hated miscarriages. They meant someone's hopes were being crushed. He took a deep breath and entered the cubicle where a woman was quietly weeping.

Oh my God. "Jen?" He took two quick steps to the gurney and clasped her hand.

Jenny squeezed his hand tightly, and her crying increased. "Cade, I'm losing our baby." A nurse handed her a tissue, and she wiped her eyes. "None of you even knew I was pregnant. We were waiting until I was at twelve weeks." She sniffed. "And now it's gone."

Caden said to the nurse, "She's a friend. You need to get someone else in here."

"Don't leave me." Jenny squeezed his hand more tightly. She was becoming more hysterical.

"I'm not going anywhere, but I can't treat you." As the nurse was leaving, he said, "Get OB down here." He reached for the stool in the corner and sat next to Jenny's head. "Where's Rob?"

"He's in Chicago."

Dammit. Caden remembered Rob had told him about the quick trip he was taking. "Does he know you're here? When's he coming home?"

"His flight was at eleven. He doesn't know." She sobbed. "Everything was fine when he left on Wednesday." She hiccupped through her tears. "He kissed my belly goodbye."

As she tried to catch her breath, Caden stroked her forehead.

"I was spotting yesterday, and I went to my doctor. They told me it wasn't unexpected. I talked to Robbie last night and told him about it. He wanted to come home, and I told him he didn't need to because the baby and I were fine. A little while ago, I had a huge cramp then this gush of blood. He was already in the air. I can't leave a voicemail telling him I'm losing our baby." Her voice broke.

Caden continued to stroke her forehead. *Where's OB? God, now I know what the patients are going through when we make them wait.* "Jen, I'm going to find a doctor. I'll be right back." He walked out and almost ran into the nurse. "Where's OB? She needs to be seen."

"They're short today, and they're all with dealing with deliveries. Someone should be down in half an hour. She was bleeding heavily when she arrived. OB won't make a difference."

Caden closed his eyes and took a deep breath. "I know." He walked back in and resumed his place at Jenny's head. "It's going to be about thirty minutes."

"Because they're all delivering babies." Her crying had subsided, but it started again. "I know there's nothing to be done." She grabbed Caden's hand. "This was our only embryo. The only one. Our only chance. And now it's gone."

When obstetrics arrived, the doctor said he wanted to do a D&C immediately. "You're bleeding profusely. This is the best course of action."

Jenny nodded. While she waited for the paperwork she need-ed to sign, she said, "Robbie lands at two thirty. Will you call him? Let him know what's going on. I'm so sorry to ask you to do that."

"Jenny, I'd do anything for you two."

At two thirty, Caden made one of the hardest calls of his life. All he had to say was that Jenny was in the hospital, and Robbie knew.

Thirty minutes later, Robbie walked into the emergency de-partment, his eyes red rimmed.

Caden's shift was done, and he met him in the hallway. "I'm so sorry. I wish there were something I could have done."

He put his arms around his friend, and Robbie remained silent while his shoulders shook from his sobs.

Finally, Robbie pulled away and took a deep, shuddering breath. "I can't break down like that in front of her. Where is she?"

Caden walked with him to the recovery room and watched as two of his closest friends embraced each other, trying to navigate their heartbreak.

Chapter Twenty-Five

Heartbreak and Healing

Jenny

A WEEK HAD PASSED since that terrible day in the emergency department. Jen stepped out of the shower and assessed her body. The bleeding had trickled to almost nothing, and her breasts were nearly back to normal. She pulled on leggings and a tank top. This was the first time Robbie had left her since she'd been released from the hospital. He promised to be home by lunchtime, and as much as she had needed him home, she was glad to have a few hours to herself.

Her mother had offered to come from Minnesota, but Jen had told her she didn't need to. Her sister, Bethany, hadn't bothered to ask. She just showed up at their door, cooked all of Jen's favorite dishes from childhood, and listened as Jen told her every detail of what they'd gone through. Beth had been twenty when Jenny met Robbie, and she had quickly declared him her honorary brother. The affection went both ways, and Jen suspected Robbie had confided his heartbreak to Bethany while he tried to maintain a stoic facade with her. Beth had left after three days but extracted a promise from her sister that she and Robbie would visit soon.

Jen made a cup of tea and went to their backyard. She remembered Robbie resting his hands on her belly the night before he left for Chicago.

"She's the size of a raspberry right now," he had told her. The embryo's development had fascinated him. Every day, he tracked it and was convinced they were having a girl.

Jenny hadn't been sure she wanted to find out the gender before she gave birth, and Robbie was certain he wanted to know. But he was willing to leave it up to her. He had wanted whatever Jenny wanted, and for those two months that she was carrying their baby, he treated her like a princess. He was so happy she was pregnant. *Then my body let us down.* Tears welled in her eyes, and she angrily brushed them away. *I'm done crying.*

Her office had told her to take two weeks off, but she was thinking about returning sooner. Their house, where she and

Robbie had talked about what the nursery would look like, seemed extra empty to her, and she didn't want to be there.

A knock sounded on the door, and when she opened it, Maureen Brady was standing there holding a container. Jenny knew it must be the cookies she was known for. She tried to remember if Caden's mother had ever been to their house. Maureen thought of Robbie as another son, but their interactions were always at Sean and Maureen's penthouse or at Cade's brownstone. "Maureen, it's lovely to see you."

The older woman placed the container she was holding on the entryway table and wrapped her arms around Jen. "Oh, my darling girl. Sean and I are so sorry for what you're going through."

Jen hadn't thought she needed her mother, but Maureen's words and her embrace flooded her with warmth she didn't realize she'd been missing. Tears welled again, but her heart filled with the maternal love from Maureen.

She let Maureen hold her for what seemed like forever, then finally, she backed away. "I was having some tea. Would you like a cup?"

When they settled in the backyard, Maureen said, "I don't think you know this. I had a miscarriage between Cathleen and Chrissy."

Jen's eyes widened. "I *didn't* know that. Do Cade and the girls know? He hasn't said anything."

"I'm sure he doesn't feel it's his story to tell. None of them knew at the time. Cade was only eleven, Claire was twelve, and of course, Chloe and Cathleen were even younger. It was too much." Maureen snorted. "Honestly, it was too much for Sean and me. When the kids got older and asked why we waited so long to have Chrissy, we told them."

"I'm so sorry. This is the worst thing I've ever gone through. I can't imagine trying to process it while tending to other children." Jenny tilted her head. "Or did that make it easier?" She grimaced. "I don't mean to be insensitive."

Maureen took her hand. "Oh, sweetheart, you're not insensitive. But there was nothing easy about it. Even with four children, Sean and I were devastated. That baby who grew in my belly for nine weeks was loved as much as any of the others."

"I was at eight weeks. She was real to us." She grinned. "Robbie was convinced it was a girl."

"Sean and I are sure the baby we lost was the brother Cade always wanted."

"How do we get over this?" Tears flowed down Jen's cheeks, and she let them. "I'm so sad."

"You'll never get over it." Maureen squeezed her hand. "Gradually, it will hurt less and less, and you'll know that for two months, that baby knew nothing but love. You and Rob have an extraordinary relationship, and you'll weather this. When are you going back to work?"

"I have another week off, but I may go back on Monday." She shook her head. "I don't want to be here."

"I understand. Sean and I would like to offer you our place in Florida. A change of scene can work wonders."

"How did you know we've talked about that?" Jenny managed to smile. "Last summer, we went to a cottage in New Hampshire, and we thought about seeing if it was available."

"Some time away from all the well-meaning people who don't know what to say will help. Three weeks after we lost our baby, we just couldn't be home any longer. Couldn't pretend that everything was fine. So we loaded the kids into the car and went to Old Orchard Beach. We ate lobsters and saltwater taffy, collected shells, and while Caden and his sisters played in the waves, Sean and I sat on the beach, and we healed. We thought maybe a few days in Florida could do the same for you and Rob."

"I'll talk to him and let you know." She studied the older woman. "How did you dare to try again? I'm so afraid."

"It wasn't easy. For several years, we thought our four would be it. We got careless one night, and three weeks later, I knew I was pregnant. I was scared to death. I obsessed over every cramp and twinge for the entire nine months."

Jen shook her head. "If it could happen like that, I might be okay. But it's not going to." She gazed at Maureen, trying to gauge how much she knew. "Robbie's sperm count is low. We did IVF."

"I knew you'd had some difficulty but not the exact cause. Cade didn't betray Rob's confidence."

"It's such a process, and I didn't react well to the hormones. I haven't told Robbie, but I'm not sure I want to try again."

Maureen stood and opened her arms to Jenny. "You and Rob have so much to offer, even if you don't give birth to a child. I know in my soul there are children out there for you to love."

"You know how we talked about getting away?"

Robbie had found Jenny on the couch when he got home. He sat beside her and brought her legs onto his lap. "Yes. I haven't asked Doug if his cottage is available, but I will if you're serious." He paused. "I wasn't sure... Do you think it will be difficult being there? We were so hopeful last summer. I'm sorry. I don't mean to..."

Jenny put her finger over his lips. "Don't apologize. I've had the same thought. Maureen came to see me this morning. She had a miscarriage between Cathleen and Chrissy."

"Wow. I didn't know that. She can relate, then. Was it helpful talking to her?"

"It was. She offered us their place in Florida." Jenny described Maureen's escape to the beach. "I like the idea of a change of scenery."

"So do I." Robbie smiled and picked up his phone. "When do you want to leave?" He started looking at flights.

Half an hour later, Jenny stuffed a pair of shorts into her carry-on. "I think that should be enough for a week. Is this crazy?"

Robbie had purchased tickets for a flight early the next morning, and a call to Maureen had provided the code for the house. "We haven't done anything spontaneous since you stopped taking the pill. It's been almost two years. A break will be good. And when we come back, we'll be ready to try again."

As he was taking the bags downstairs, a knock sounded on the door.

Robbie opened it to find Danny. "Dan, hi." He hadn't seen Danny alone since the night he hit him.

Jenny stepped to Robbie's side. "Hi, Danny." She knew he'd spent two nights at Caden's brownstone while she was in the hospital, losing the baby, and that he'd quit his job. Brooke told her he was back home, but she described things as tense.

"Can I... Can I come in?"

"Of course." Jenny clutched Robbie's arm with one hand and motioned Danny in with the other.

"Cade told me what happened. Well, of course Brooke did as well. I'm so sorry." His face was a mask of sadness.

"Thanks. It's a disappointment. That's for sure."

Jenny missed the easy banter that Robbie and Danny used to have.

"Are you going somewhere?" He was looking at their bags.

"Maureen and Sean offered us the use of their house in Florida. We just need to get away."

"I get that." He blew out a long breath. "You know I left my job?" When they nodded, he continued, "Maybe I need to get away too. But hey, I didn't come to whine about me. I wanted to be sure you knew how sorry I am. You're so great with Liam. If anyone deserves to have kids, it's you guys, and I'm pissed on your behalf." That was a hint of the Danny they knew, fiery and loyal to a fault.

Robbie chuckled. "Thanks. That means a lot."

Danny threw his arms around Robbie. "And back in the fall, I was out of line."

"Not my finest moment either."

Danny let go of Robbie, turned to Jenny, took her hands, and kissed her cheek. "I'm rooting for you."

The Bradys' home in Florida was a huge departure from the northeast. Tropical flowers adorned the manicured lawn, and towering palms swayed in the breeze. The house was immense, with room for all the Bradys to gather plus a casita for more space.

Jenny shook her head as they explored. "This is beautiful, but we're going to get lost. Leave it to Maureen to have everything be top-shelf."

The week passed with long walks on the beach, breakfast beside the pool, leisurely dinners at a different restaurant every night, laughing together like Jenny remembered, and falling asleep in each other's arms. They pointedly avoided anything having to do with fertility.

On their last day, they lounged by the pool, and Jenny said, "I feel much more like me. I'm glad we came. Are you?"

"I am." He sat up and faced Jenny. "What are we going to do when we get back? Let's talk about using donor sperm." He took her hand in his. "We could do IUI and have a greater chance of success. That would be less stress on you."

"Are you saying that because you think it's important to me to carry our baby?"

Robbie rubbed his jaw. "Isn't it?"

"I thought it was. But that was when I thought it would be *our* baby. If we use donor sperm..."

"I know. It won't be mine. I've come to peace with that."

"I'm not sure I have. I want to pursue adoption."

"Now?" He had a hint of a smile on his face.

"Yes. We always said we would adopt. I think now is the time to get going on that. I can't do IVF again, Robbie."

"You're really okay with not going through a pregnancy? With not nursing?"

"I'm totally okay with it. There may be some residual sadness, but having to put my body through the hormone deluge for IVF, not getting any embryos, then only getting one and losing that baby after eight weeks—it was awful. I can't do it. I'm sorry."

"Darlin', don't be sorry. We want to be parents, and we're going to get there."

Epilogue

Quinn

MEMORIES FLOODED OVER QUINN as she spread her towel on the sand between Brooke and Jen. The last time she'd been on Old Orchard Beach, she was days away from leaving for college and convinced she would spend the rest of her life with Sam Carpenter. Within months, that relationship had imploded, and Quinn had spent years searching for someone to love who would love her back. Three years ago, she'd realized what she really needed was to love herself. A moratorium on dating had given her the time to do that, and she'd become totally content with her life in rural New Hampshire. Then Caden Brady had stolen her heart. Their road had not always been smooth, but their connection was deep, and in a week, they would pledge to love each other forever.

Quinn's friends, her tribe in New Hampshire, had taken her to a spa as her bachelorette weekend. Brooke and Jen wanted to do something different to celebrate Quinn and had decided on a trip to the ocean. Brooke had been the interior designer when a luxury hotel nearby was redecorated two years ago and had been offered a complimentary suite. Check-in wasn't until four, so they agreed to meet at the beach.

Quinn was the last to arrive, and while she was excited to spend a weekend in the lap of luxury, she wasn't as comfortable with her new friends as she had been with the women from New Hampshire. And both Brooke and Jen had things going on in their lives that could make the weekend awkward.

Quinn sank onto her towel. "The last time I was here was almost twelve years ago." She looked around and laughed. "It hasn't changed much. The boardwalk looks as weatherworn now as it did then."

Jen said, "This is my first time. When I was in college, we went to Cape Cod, and Robbie and I continued that after we got married. We've been to Portland and Bar Harbor but never here."

"The Cape fits you better." Quinn smiled. "How about you, Brooke?"

"Danny and Liam came up for a weekend when I was working on Water's Edge. We brought Liam over here one afternoon. He loved it." Brooke was more subdued than usual.

Anything having to do with Danny would be a touchy subject, so Quinn scrambled to find a neutral topic, hoping for something Brooke was excited about. "Did you finish that penthouse for Trinity Gammish? Caden and I had dinner with her this week. She's super nice."

Brooke's face flushed. "No, it's not done yet. She's one of those clients making changes as we go along, and that always slows things down." She took a deep breath, and her face returned to its normal color. "And that increases the cost, but it's not an issue for her. It's going to be so gorgeous." She sighed. "Is she coming to the wedding?"

"I think so. She wasn't on our initial guest list, but Caden added her at the last minute." Quinn opened the app on her phone where she was tracking responses to their wedding invitations. "Yes, she's coming by herself. Cade said a major reason she left California was because the relationship she'd been in since she got there had ended. I'm not sure if she's still recovering from that or if she just hasn't found someone. Anyway, no plus-one for her."

"I can't wait to meet this paragon." Jen sat up and reapplied sunscreen. "I've still got a little tan left from our week in Florida, but I don't want to burn."

"The week away helped?" Quinn hadn't seen her since she and Robbie had returned ten days earlier.

"It did. Everyone at home—colleagues, friends—knew what had happened. So when we saw them for the first time, of course, they wanted to tell us how sorry they were. Our emotions were so raw that it was hard to have it in our face all the time." She looked stricken. "I'm not talking about you guys. Your support meant so much. But in Florida, no one knew us, so we could move beyond it. At least for some brief periods of time. Maureen and Sean's house is beautiful, and the landscaping is spectacular." She described the tropical flowers and the palm trees. "We loved it, but we both decided we liked the place we went to last year on Lake Winnipesaukee better. It had a rustic charm."

"Do you want to talk about what you're going to do next? If you don't want to, I understand."

"I don't mind. We're going to start the adoption process. Our first meeting for our home study is next week."

"No more IVF? I thought you wanted to carry a baby. Will you get a baby if you adopt?" Brooke slathered on sunscreen. "I know very little about adoption."

"We won't do IVF again. It was hard in so many ways. On my body and on our mental health. Losing our baby was devastating, and I can't go through it again. Obviously, we'd like a newborn. We've also got appointments with a couple of agencies to see what the best direction to take is." She adjusted her bathing suit straps. "It's almost four. Should we head to the hotel? I can't wait to see this place." After pausing, she continued, "Don't feel sorry for us. We're at peace with this decision and excited to get started. Quinn, you may not know this, but Robbie and I have always intended to adopt. It's just going to happen more quickly than we imagined."

When they entered the hotel suite, Quinn gasped. They were facing French doors that looked out on the ocean. Three of the walls were a warm eggshell color, and the other was paneling painted marine blue. The furniture was in shades of oyster white and blue, accented with nautical-themed pillows. It was a three-bedroom suite, giving them each their own space. "Brooke, this is gorgeous." She grinned. "When Sam and I came here before I left for college, we stayed at a campground in a tiny orange tent that was just big enough for the two of us. This is certainly different."

"It was a fun project." Brooke looked wistful. "Let's unpack then have a glass of wine out on the balcony. Our dinner reservation isn't until seven."

On the balcony, Jenny asked about the wedding, and Quinn shared what she and Caden had planned.

"He was having such a difficult time trying to decide between Danny and Rob for best man. And I was having the same issue with my closest friends. We didn't want to hurt anyone's feelings."

"I know Robbie understands," Jenny replied.

Brooke's phone rang before she could speak up. "It's Danny." She stepped into the living room.

Quinn sipped her wine then looked at Jennifer. "The situation with Danny is the elephant in the room. I feel like I need to say something. Especially since Caden played such a huge role."

"She's not doing a very good job of hiding the turmoil she's feeling. Maybe if we get her talking about it, her mood will improve."

Brooke came back. "Rob is with them, and Liam has him making Legos." She took a swallow of her wine. "I was concerned that Danny wouldn't get to the house on time. It's the first time he's been back. Other than when he came to pick up Liam and Tally."

After spending two nights with Caden, Danny had returned home and told Brooke about quitting his job. A couple of days later, he met with Arnie to hammer out the details of the new position. Arnie intended to expand to have more accounts in Boston, and Danny would be the contact person for those, but currently, the bulk of his business was in New Hampshire. He'd be okay with Danny working remotely eventually but wanted him to be in New Hampshire for at least the first six months. One of his accounts was a ski resort, and he had arranged for Danny to have a suite of rooms. Danny had shared all the details with Caden, including his thought that time apart might be what he and Brooke needed. After clearing it with Quinn,

Caden had offered him Quinn's townhouse for as long as he wanted it.

Caden and Quinn helped him childproof the space, and he had moved in two weeks ago. Reluctantly, Brooke had agreed he could bring Liam and Tally to New Hampshire on the weekends, and he traveled to Boston to have dinner with them once a week. While Brooke was in Maine, Danny was with the kids in the city.

Caden was staying in close contact with him and told Quinn he was sure Danny had cut way back on his drinking. But Quinn had not talked to Brooke about the situation, and she was afraid her friend might think she and Caden were taking Danny's side.

Quinn couldn't avoid the subject any longer. "How are you handling everything?"

"I'm okay. Hiring the nanny during the winter has helped. I couldn't do it by myself otherwise." She took a deep breath. "And Danny's done exactly what we agreed to. He had the kids last weekend and came down to spend time with them on Wednesday. I can't deny he's in a better place than he has been in a long time."

"We want the best solution for both of you. Just because Danny's in my townhouse doesn't mean—"

"You don't have to say it. Cade has talked to me. You know that, right?"

"Yes, I know." *Does she think Caden isn't going to tell me he's seen her? One of our most sacred promises to each other is that we won't keep secrets.*

At the restaurant, they enjoyed lobster and ordered a second bottle of wine. Brooke finally relaxed, and they all giggled as they talked about going to baseball games.

Jen drained her glass of wine and said to Quinn, "I have to tell you something."

Brooke breathed, "Oh God."

"What? She needs to know."

Quinn looked from one woman to the other. "You're making me nervous."

"Last Fourth of July, Robbie and I were walking from the waterfront to Danny and Brooke's house, and I think I saw Mary."

"Caden's Mary?" Quinn asked cautiously.

"Don't call her that," Brooke said indignantly.

"Yes," Jen answered. "The bitch that Caden was supposed to marry."

"Okay. Did you talk to her?"

"God no. But Quinn, she was holding hands with a guy, and he had a small child on his shoulders. Maybe three years old. With curly black hair."

"Like Caden's." Quinn's stomach twisted. "Are you saying you think it's Caden's child?"

"I don't know. But it could be."

"Have you told him?"

"No. You guys were so happy when you returned from Honduras and I didn't want to drop it on him. Time passed and I haven't known how or if I even should."

"So you told me. What the hell am I going to do with it? I can't tell him. He'd be crushed to think he has a child out there and that he's missed out on three years of its life. But... how can I *not* tell him?"

Quinn looked between the two women again, and they both shrugged.

The table was quiet for several minutes, then Brooke said, "I kissed Trinity Gammish."

Afterword

DID YOU ENJOY THIS book? If you did, leaving a review on Amazon or Goodreads is a wonderful way to let the author know. Reviews are one of the most powerful tools in an author's arsenal.

Sneak Peak

AT TRUE NORTH ADOPTION Agency in northern Vermont

After dinner, Robbie led Jenny outside. "Let's explore." Flower gardens filled with bright blooms surrounded the house, and he could see stone walls bordering the tree line. They spent more than an hour walking through the woods, following the impeccably groomed paths, and ended up at a fire pit.

"Do you know how to turn that on?" Jenny asked as she tugged Robbie toward a double lounge chair.

He reached for a switch, and the fire pit sprang to life. They settled on the chair, and Robbie pulled Jenny's legs over his. "This is quite a place."

"I know. I wish I were some kind of artist so I could come to a retreat and paint in that conservatory." She sighed. "But seriously, without even hearing their presentation tomorrow, I understand why they have such positive reviews. Ellie was so kind and the services they offer to pregnant women. Can you imagine if the young girls living on the streets in Boston had access to a program like this?" She shook her head.

"Umm," Robbie murmured as he lowered his mouth to her neck. After nuzzling her, he pulled back. "Are you going to tell me what happened between you and Brooke last night?"

"I was pissed at how she ignored us at Caden's wedding, and I let her know."

"I knew you were."

"It's more than the wedding." Jenny studied him for several seconds. "When we went to Maine a few weeks ago, she told Quinn and me that she had kissed Trinity. That's her client's name."

Robbie opened his eyes wider. "Seriously?"

"Yes. Our friendship, the tight bond we have, is disappearing, and I feel like whatever Brooke has going on with Trinity is a big factor in that."

"Are they... you know?" He motioned with his hands.

Jenny snorted. "I don't think so, but who knows? She's acting so differently from the woman I've known almost as long as I've known you. She called me a bitch."

"Oh babe. I'm sorry."

"I feel like I'm a homophobe, but honestly, it won't be the same hanging out with her and Trinity instead of her and Danny. It won't be the same no matter who she's with. And I feel bad for Danny. I know he put her through hell, but now he's trying to get himself back together, and I don't know if she even cares. It kills me to think of Liam and Tally having to shuttle between their parents. Everything is just a mess."

Robbie pulled her closer to him. "It is. I know. All we can do is support both of them." He felt her relax against him, and he buried his head in her hair and rubbed circles on her back, willing the tension she'd been carrying to disappear.

"Looks like we're interrupting some lovebirds."

Robbie jerked his head up as the words spoken in an English accent split the silence of the night. Two men were standing on the opposite side of the fire pit. One was lean and had dark hair sprinkled with gray. The other was a burly black man. He was as tall as Robbie and probably fifty pounds heavier. Robbie thought they were at least five years older than he and Jenny.

"Sorry to interrupt you, mate." That English accent appeared again, coming from the larger man, and Robbie wondered if they were both British.

"No big deal. Are you here for the get-acquainted weekend?"

The smaller man answered, without a trace of the English accent. "Yes." He was carrying a bottle and two glasses. "Care to join us for a drink?"

"We don't have glasses. But thanks for the offer."

The British man walked to a cabinet that Robbie had not noticed, opened it and removed two glasses. "Problem solved. Now you can join us."

Jenny cocked her head. "You've been here before." It was a statement, not a question.

"This is our second go-round, darling." He drew out the word, and Robbie winked at Jenny.

"All right. What was that look between you two?"

"He likes to call me darling." Jenny giggled. "But the accent is Southern, not English."

"Let's hear it." When Robbie blushed and looked questioningly at Jenny, the man said, "Come on now. Dahhling. Can you match that?" The accent was more pronounced than it had been before.

Robbie grinned, shaking his head. "Darlin'."

"Ooh," The other man said, "that's pretty hot, Arch."

The British man guffawed. "Fuck you." He crossed the distance to Robbie and Jenny with the bottle and glasses in hand. "I'm Archer, and that traitor is my husband, Anton." He filled the glasses with amber liquid and passed them to the couple.

Robbie extended his free hand. "Thanks. I'm Rob, and this is my wife, Jenny."

They shook hands, and Archer returned to sit beside his husband. "I'm not hearing southern. Do you use it only when it suits your purpose? Mine's the real deal."

Jenny answered with a smile. "He's strategic about it. Tell us about your experience here. Have you adopted already?"

Anton pulled out his phone and found a picture. "That's our daughter Mya. She'll be four in the fall and wants a sibling. So here we are."

Jenny sighed as she looked at the picture of a mixed-race girl with long dark curls and a wide smile. "She's beautiful."

Archer replied without a hint of the teasing sarcasm he'd used before. "She's the most special thing in the world to us. What do you want to know?"

"Everything. We don't know what we don't know."

Robbie inserted, "Let's start with how long it took you. Was Mya a newborn when you got her?"

Anton and Archer exchanged glances, and Anton said, "Go ahead." He looked at Robbie. "He's the bigger talker between us."

"Never would have figured that out." Robbie chuckled.

"Our story is not typical. We came to a get-acquainted weekend four years ago. Started the process, you'll get all the details about that tomorrow, and then, we got lucky. We have a restaurant in Providence, and I had a teenage girl, Lanny, working as a dishwasher. One night she collapsed, and I had her transported to the hospital. After we closed for the night, I went to check on her. Found out she was pregnant and had been living on the streets. I took her home with me, and she stayed until her baby was born."

Anton spoke up. "Imagine the scene. Archer comes home with this waif, who probably hadn't had a hot shower in days. What the fuck were we going to do with her? I had to remind him we wanted a baby, not a teenager."

Archer reached for his hand, and the affection between them radiated like a beacon. "Lanny was a runaway and there was more than one candidate for fatherhood, all of whom denied the baby was theirs. She had no one in her corner."

Anton broke in again. "She blossomed with us. Insisted she could keep working, and she did, right up until two days before the baby was born."

"Our profile with True North was active and we'd had one possible match, but it didn't work out. That wasn't unexpected, but it was disappointing. Lanny asked us to be in the delivery room with her. She told us we'd been more like parents to her in the three months she was with us than her own mother and father had ever been."

"Most moving experience of my life." Anton put his hand over his heart. "You can't imagine watching this tiny eighteen-year-old girl push a baby out into the world."

"And when she had time to catch her breath, she told us the baby was ours. Unbeknownst to us, she was fully aware that we were trying to adopt and had decided we would be the best parents for Mya."

"The people at True North were amazing. They stepped in to support not just us but Lanny as well. She stayed with us for six months, got her GED, enrolled in community college and moved into an apartment. The adoption is completely open, and Mya knows she grew in Lanny's belly.

"Lanny moved to New Mexico last year with her boyfriend. She stays in touch, but not as heavily as in the first few years."

"She knows she'll always have a place with us, though. We didn't just adopt a baby, we symbolically took on a young adult too."

"Wow." Jenny's eyes were glowing. "That's a great story."

"Just remember, darling, our experience was not the norm."

Robbie and Jenny and Danny and Brooke's stories continue in Whispers of Family coming in November, 2025.

Acknowledgements

This one took a lot of research as I strove to portray the medical details of a fertility journey. Part of my research involved listening to Unexpecting, the podcast of Tara Lipinski and her husband Todd Kapostasy. They struggled for five years and finally welcomed their daughter, born via surrogacy in 2023. Tara and Todd will never know me but I'm grateful to them for their honesty, humor and strength in exposing their vulnerability to the world.

Unexpecting led me to other podcasts and another one that entered my listening rotation was The eggwhisperer Show with Dr. Aimee Eyvazzadeh. I learned a tremendous amount about so many aspects of infertility by listening to Dr. Aimee and I'm grateful to her and others who seek to educate.

Emily Hensley of Small Fry Marketing offers critical support in so many ways, including my website and my covers.

I'm thankful for my wonderful team of ARC readers who review my books and promote me on social media, both areas that an author can't ignore in today's world.

My husband Gordy has lit up my life since the day we spent in the kiddie lit section of our college library.

And always, Thank you to my readers for spending some of your precious time reading my books.

Also by

Whispers of Goodbye
Whispers of Forgiveness
Whispers of Mistletoe
Whispers of Starlight
Whispers of Healing
Whispers of Change
Whispers of Humility

About the author

SUE IS AN AVID reader who ventured into the writing world during the first year of the Pandemic. Her stories showcase men and women working to become whole and happy. Family plays a prominent role as do the steamy encounters which come with falling in love.

Sue is a lifelong Vermonter who counts books, sunsets, and travel as vital to her being. Mountains, from the slopes of Vermont's Greens to the towering peaks of Colorado's Rockies feed her soul.

Her children are grown and flown and she's living her happily ever after with the boy she met in a college library fifty years ago.

Follow her on Facebook, Sue Mills – Author

Or on her website, suemillsauthor.com

Or on Instagram, suemillsauthor

SUE MILLS

And TikTok, Sue Mills, Author